NEIL CAMPBELL is from M
four times in *Best British Sho*
Sky Hooks was published in
of short stories published, a

NEIL CAMPBELL

LICENSED PREMISES

SALT
MODERN
STORIES

SALT

CROMER

PUBLISHED BY SALT PUBLISHING 2022

2 4 6 8 10 9 7 5 3 1

First published in Great Britain in 2022 by
Salt Publishing Ltd
12 Norwich Road, Cromer, Norfolk NR27 0AX United Kingdom

www.saltpublishing.com

Salt Publishing Limited Reg. No. 5293401

A CIP catalogue record for this book is available from the British Library

ISBN 978 1 78463 250 2 (Paperback edition)
ISBN 978 1 78463 251 9 (Electronic edition)

Typeset in Granjon by Salt Publishing

Printed and bound in Great Britain by Clays Ltd, Elcograf S.p.A *for Mum*

Contents

Jackdaws

A GIANT BLACK crucifix was chained to one of the rocks, and there was a laminated sheet of paper stapled to the wood with black type on it and a photograph of the girl.

One morning I walked out into a blizzard and the snow on the doorstep reached my kneecaps. The gritters from the council didn't come until the day before the snow melted, meaning all the cars on the lane had to be parked outside the pub for almost a month. The jackdaws stood out against the snow-covered hillsides, and the drystone walls cut the sloping fields into segments.

When the sun finally came out after a month the white-clothed trees around the cricket ground sparkled. Blackbirds and song thrushes spilled white dust from the branches and silver drops fell off the leaves. The Churn was an alpine peak rolling over to a similarly submerged Far Head. The Pike shimmered in a covering of carbuncles.

As the snow melted and the sun retreated, the water froze in sheets of ice along the lane, descending like a toboggan run at the corner near the footpath for the allotments.

There were yellow sand buckets at each end of the lane but the sand soon ran out.

I was standing by the back door with a steaming cup of tea, looking at the clough when I heard a rumbling from above. A block of snow came sliding down off my sloped roof, landing on the communal pathway and rising halfway up my back window. As I shovelled some of it out of the way I saw that in the field beyond the drystone wall, two kids in red jackets had made a ski jump out of the snow and were snowboarding down the hillside, spiralling in the air.

From the council estate I walked up past the pig farm, climbed up a grassy hill filled with sheep and a couple of hares and reached the top road through a stile built into the drystone wall. I looked down on the village, the tiny circle of the cricket ground and the oblong of the football pitch, the two bisected by the grey line of the footpath that led from the footbridge over the A road and across to where the old red phone box stood next to the post box in the wall.

The Dark Peak was transformed by summer. The blooming of so many trees constituted that change. As I looked across the valley, I could see what happened every July. The field behind my house was a bright yellow, the rape enclosed in its drystone box and made a dazzling golden yellow by the sun sinking through it.

Turning my back to the view from the top road, I went left and through a grey gate and made a gradual ascent of the bridleway, looking to my left across to the moorland, the A road winding in the foreground paralleled by the train line.

Going through a tiny gate in the drystone wall that had been completely buried by a snow drift the previous winter, I turned right across the moorland, across shifting sphagnum moss and a hollow from where I could see horses on one side and black cows on the other. I walked uphill to a T-junction of faint footpaths, from where I could look out towards Far Head and The Pike. A single raven spiralled in the up draught, showing the purple in its feathers.

Dropping down, I followed the footpath and sat on a bench, looking across towards the tiny cars on the road far below, heading downhill towards New Town.

The rain had been coming down hard for a week. The cricket ground was a lake, the football pitch reduced to a peninsula and the path between the two impassable. Water ran east to west down the lane, the slight descent of the tarmac and the drystone walls either side funnelling it. Cars with bright headlights sloshed to work and back, the postwoman waded through the water, wheeling her trolley of post and stopping every now and then to wipe the rain from her glasses.

The top of The Churn was cloaked in cloud. Far Head was also concealed by the mist. The trains passed by within sound, not sight. The traffic on the A road splashed in a heightened roar. The electricity pylons reached up into the grey, their tops lost to the cloud, and jackdaws huddled on the wires.

The rain had been sluicing down off the clough and was blocked at the back by the drystone wall, until the water escaped by going under it and re-emerging like a spring through one of the paving stones in the yard. From there it collected in a dip in the concrete and came in a channel towards the house, sloshing down the concrete steps by the back door. Thankfully there was a drain on the communal pathway that passed by the back of all the houses of the terrace, and most of the water splashed its way down into that. But then even the drain started to back up and the water became a pond by the back door, getting closer and closer to the lip of the doorway with each day of cloud and rain.

I'd been told about the flood in the 1980s, when the water board had been doing something and the drains had been blocked. Water came running off the clough and flooded the houses on the lane on its way into the brook. The water ran from the pond in the farmyard with the flag of St George above it, and under the houses on the lane, and below the cricket pitch and the A road before re-emerging by the pub.

This time the drains stood up to the strain and after a couple of days of grey cloud but no more rain the water levels in the back yard lowered. The river that had been forming in a rush towards my back door was reduced to a mere stream, and the stream seemed to be escaping down the drain without too big a pond forming on the communal concrete pathway.

Brave enough to risk opening the back door I stood there and saw that the water line no longer reached for the lip of the door frame. All was silent save the sound of running water, and as each day passed that sound reduced in volume until a gentle trickle was lost to the traffic noise off the bypass. I thought I was through it, and I watched a grey heron flapping past the garden shed on its way over the pond where the frogmen had been.

I jumped on the train. Getting off I walked up the hill and away from the town in the direction of the moss, before crossing the road and going up the steep grassy bank. Climbers hung from the rocks below me as I looked across the valley to the reservoir. I could hear the cries of the children at the secondary school.

I followed the track along the edge, looking over the drystone wall on my left to the fields of cotton grass swaying on the moss. The music of meadow pipits and swallows played all around as I sat at the head of a grassy descent. That music was joined by the troubled-sounding calls of curlews that echoed from the brook. Through the binoculars I watched their grey-winged flapping and listened to the calls that punctuated the continued music of the meadow pipits and the whistling swallows. I thought of the soft ground beneath the swaying white of the cotton grass fields, and the screaming of the children seemed to rise.

Walking down the hill and cutting through the farm I headed into the neighbouring village, passing the pub there and carrying on along the road until taking a footpath to the right that followed a tunnel under the train line and led to the shores of the reservoir. The dampened path led through trees and alongside the watery ditch of the brook still running down the valley in parallel. That water was blocked from view save for silver shafts of light through the trees.

There were voices of people I couldn't see and I thought maybe they were fishermen, but when I reached the northern end of the reservoir and looked across the water, I could see it was a group of men in red canoes. They looked tiny in the expanse of silver water that reflected the shoreline trees. I thought of the depths below the still surface. Above all stood the bulk of the moss, and the long ridge line with the cotton grass still blowing.

On the lane out of the village there was a caravan covered in ivy with sagging bin liners outside it surrounded by flies. In the yellow light shining in through the back window of the caravan there was a bearded man surrounded by swirling smoke, with two black dogs barking beside him. He smiled knowingly as I passed.

I came up a green hillside that was scattered with sheep wool hanging on to thistles below a sky filled with jackdaws. I crossed the road and passed another farm to stand and gaze at the familiar bulk of The Churn, the dominant hillside brightened, made golden by sunlight breaking through cloud.

The trees in the woods grew thick and rose up to the road-side. They shadowed the steady run of the river as it flowed towards the reservoir. Looking across from the reservoir, the trees of the woods looked collected, condensed, their branches shadowing the undergrowth. In winter, that foot-path up through the trees was often bright with moonlight, the sparkle of the stars and the orb of the moon casting a pale glow on the mulch of leaves and weeds.

Above the whitewashed walls of a farmhouse, and beside where the jackdaws roosted in the trees, I stood on the road and watched a rustling in the undergrowth. Orange poppies wobbled. And then the rabbits burst out: one, two, three of them. Two of them ran down the hill together and I watched their tails bobbing, while the other one seemed confused. It ran around in circles and then stopped, before running around in more circles and stopping again. Its feet slid on the tarmac on its turns, and when it stopped it wavered from one side to another as though on the verge of collapse. There was something strange about its eyes. I bent down to look closer and it rushed off in circles before collapsing onto the orange poppies.

The village was on the news every night for a week. Reporters stood on the path between the cricket ground and the football pitch, in front of cameras pointing towards the houses on the lane. They stood under umbrellas as the brook rose higher, and the pond continued to deepen below the flag of St George.

She was my neighbour Sheila's daughter. I'd seen her many times running past the window, often chasing some dog or other. She had blonde hair and seemed to wear pink most of the time and always had a mischievous smile on her face.

The cricket ground began to fill with floral tributes. All day people would park outside the pub and come walking across the bridge over the bypass to lay flowers and little cards with messages of support. Cars weren't allowed on the cordoned-off lane for weeks.

Sheila would walk down the lane, arm in arm with other women. She'd bend down to read the cards attached to the flowers, kneeling on the grass of the cricket ground in the shadow of The Churn. Cameramen would film the women. I noticed that Sheila didn't cry. But she rapidly lost weight, and when I walked past her on the street she scowled.

A lot of people in the village kept themselves to themselves, just like I did in many ways. In winter, particularly, it was so dark and cold that neighbours rarely saw each other anyway. There were hardly any street lights, and on cloudy nights in winter it got absolutely black, the looming bulk of The Churn indistinguishable from the black skies that surrounded it.

Just at the bottom of the lane, on the corner and near the turn-off for the footpath leading to the allotments, the road went uphill to a rusted iron gate, and beyond that in the field there was a great hole in the ground that looked like it had once been a quarry. In it there were all kinds of rubbish. I'd walked with her down the bank and into the hole and there were washing machines, a smashed and scattered Belfast sink, bags of cement, oil drums, gas canisters, prams, bikes, cracked sledges, broken kites, punctured footballs, a twisted scooter, a blue plastic cricket bat all bent, a tennis ball half sheared.

It was early, just before sunrise, with mist still rising and smells of bracken and the pig farm lingering in the windless air. I zipped my fleece and pulled my beanie hat low over my ears and tucked my gloved hands into my pockets. The front gate squeaked as I closed it. My boots scraped the tarmac on the lane. There was a pied wagtail on the cricket ground, bobbing through the mist. The occasional HGV roared along the bypass.

Leaning on the drystone wall at the bottom of the clough, below the flag of St George hanging above the pond in the farmyard, I looked up at the blackened trees, and the silver sky on which the branches were sharply outlined. The jackdaws took off for a brief sortie, swirling in the sky above the cricket ground before coming back to land in the branches of the trees. As the sun came up above The Churn, I knew it was the last time I would see them.

Oystercatchers

TURNING THE CORNER past a row of pines and walking down to the boat hut and the small wooden jetty, where two wooden skiffs float with a foot of water in them, Tom looks across the length of the lake. Geese fly in formations and there is the occasional wild cry of a buzzard. There are ducks in the reeds, a pair of grey herons, and blackbirds criss-crossing the lake from one tree to another. He rises from his seat and walks around the far rim of the lake, a place grown over from disuse, a moss of green covering the route through the forest and the tributary paths to parts of an old sawmill. He climbs over branches in the path and glimpses a hind. He passes through the reeds and fallen pines by the lake. There are ducks and geese and buzzards and lapwings and curlews and oystercatchers on the moors beyond. Wind blows through the pines. Light shines through as they sway and creak and brush together. There are dead trees too, as he emerges from under the wavering canopy, with their solid looking trunks and bare branches outlined against the moving clouds in the sky.

As he sorts through his paperwork at RC Containers, her breasts brush against his elbow.

You're always out here, aren't you? he says.

Not always.

You like a bit of rough, is that it?

She smiles again. That's what you are, is it?

Well, compared to them lot in there.

You're a bit cocky aren't you? she says, looking him up and down. Anyway I can't stay out here all day.

I bet you wish you could.

Nah, I'd rather be in there, she says, picking up the paperwork from his desk and standing there a moment before going back towards the office.

So, what's your mobile then? he asks.

In his car by the lake there's the lace of Susannah's G-string above her jeans, and the small of her back above that as she leans forward. Her seatbelt is tight between her breasts. Tom takes the seatbelt off, and before the car battery begins to get low from all the heating, she moves over onto him.

The curtains change from black to grey. A song thrush goes through its repertoire. Tom opens the curtains. Sociable jackdaws fill the telegraph wires. Coal tits and sparrows bicker in the air beside the feeder.

He thinks of them in the parked car, and how she played with the ring on her finger. He didn't see the NO PARKING sign, and after they had been there for about an hour, an old man came out of his house. He knocked on the window and said, there's no parking here, and, can't you read? Can't you see the sign?

Tom goes into the estate agents and looks at various properties, one next to a church with a belted Yew tree. He drives up the road out of the village, higher and higher so that in his rear view mirror the viaduct leading over the river looks tiny. At the crest of the hill he stops in a parking space. The road stretches in curls across the moorland. Drainage channels shine and there's a long row of grouse butts. The sunlight falls on a stone building sat alone on the moor surrounded by the sounds of pheasants. He drives on. Golden plovers sit above him on telegraph wires, their plumage brightened by the sun. Great congregations of starlings float by. Lapwings sound like the tuning of an old radio, and curlews whistle too. He drives back along the road over the moorland, passes the turn down the hill for the village and sits in his car looking at the river.

Turning the car around, he drives back towards the top of the moorland. The whole county stretches out below him. There's a soundtrack of curlews and lapwings and oystercatchers as he drives down the hill to the village. He thinks of her breasts brushing his elbow. He sees another man kissing them, playing with them. He thinks of her enjoying it.

They meet in the car by the bridge over the river and he drives them across the A road. They carry on up the road in silence. At a parking space overlooking the moorland, he puts his hand on her thigh and looks into her eyes.

Look, I've been looking at houses for us. We can live high up on the moors where nobody will know us, imagine it? We—

—Slow down. *We?* she says, her eyes not meeting his.

Please, Susannah, he says, passing her a poem as grouse on the moorland fly over butts.

What about the children? she asks.

What do you mean?

I mean, what about the children?

In a field among sheep, there are long shadows of trees and the calls of buzzards and kestrels and curlews and lapwings. Tom walks down to the banks of the river, where there's a man standing in the water with the current.

Although he doesn't have a permit, one day Tom takes a fishing rod across the fields and steps into the river. While casting he lets the water shift him east. He flicks his line out in lazy swings casting for brown trout or salmon. Near the confluence of the two rivers, he sits down on the riverbank; the only sounds the flow of the river and the plops of feeding fish. A grey heron stands motionless on the opposite bank and then unfolds itself to disappear over tall trees. Dirt has collected in the loose skin on Tom's knuckles, stayed ridged in the hard edges of his fingers. There's a trickle of blood from his middle finger. He gets up and takes his line out of the current. At the car park he sits for a long time in the car.

A buzzard calls. Jackdaws swirl back to their nests. Highland cattle standing in the grounds of the Great Hall blink into the sun from under their fringes. Where the river sweeps in a crescent past the hall and the stepping-stones towards the woods and then on to the castle, two grey herons lift off into the evening sky.

Tom stands by the car. Faces on the westbound train disappear into the tunnel. He walks down the road in the darkness. There are more buzzards above the woods, and there's the trickle of burns flowing down from the high moorland. He passes the earthworks and the barn that houses all the tractors and farm machinery. Bats flash back and forth. Turning right he walks through the village.

He crosses a field and passes a quarry and a saw-mill before walking down to the side of the river. Great banks of stones sit dry in the middle of the water. The current runs east down either side of the stones, calm in the deepest parts, bubbling and running faster over rocks in the shallowest. Tom sits on the bank and dips his aching hands in the water, feeling the cold run over them. As the channel of water rushes over his hands the black and white feathers of the oystercatchers continue to swirl around him, the whistling from their orange beaks becoming louder and louder.

The River Through the Trees

G REG REMEMBERED HER from the barber shop. And now, seeing him on the train, she had gotten off without saying anything. He had wanted to go over but it felt pointless, so he kept his boots under the table, didn't move.

On the other side of the river the field was a sea of yellow rapeseed flowers. Another field was a weak red scattering of poppies. They passed through where the rivers met, through scenes he'd been through so many times: muddy fields filled with cows, jackdaws in the mud, footpaths by the river, men standing up to the waist in the river. On certain stretches of the line, the train seemed right above the water, and near the A road they crossed over a bridge under which he'd played as a boy. There was a woman in wellington boots walking an old greyhound, and the sound of the train caused a group of oystercatchers to come flapping from the water, peeping all the while. The A road seemed quiet, and when the train pulled into his station, pretty despite the nearby presence of the sewage works, he paused a moment to look at the birds perched on the sewage. As the train pulled away, the driver hesitant by the level crossing, Greg looked across at the castle,

and the hillsides surrounding it, and the pine plantations on the hillsides, and the sunlight, and shadows of
cloud. There were more oystercatchers peeping. He felt
himself start to shake, and then tears came, but he fought
them off.

The pub was next to the pottery, right by the village
green and the post office, with the A road high up on the
hill behind. He walked in and half-hoped for a welcome,
but the young barmaid didn't recognize him, and he didn't
recognize her, he didn't think. And then he thought maybe
she was the daughter of the landlady. He also thought she
had a glint in her eye at the sight of him. The pool table
was still there but the pub seemed tiny. It was amazing how
so many things looked the same, how nothing changed,
how you could go away and come back and for a moment
it was like you'd never been away at all. He necked two
pints and then went back through the train station and
crossed the green footbridge over the river to take the route
home past the castle. There were oystercatchers in a field
down there and he could look across the river at the backs
of houses. There would be no twitching curtains this way.
He felt most comfortable under the cover of the woods,
just the sparkle of the river through the trees. A footpath
he could walk with his eyes closed, if he wished. At a farm
gate the chain was twisted over the fence post in the same
way it always had been, and when he eventually reached
the tarmac road, he looked across at the cow shed, all their
heads lolling out from the shade, and kept walking past the
grounds of the old hall and down the long straight road to
the village. He had to stop when he saw her. The same just
with more grey hair, and still putting washing out on the

line. He said nothing until he reached the garden gate. As he opened it, the gate squeaked in the same old way, and she turned around and put a hand to her mouth.

He took his seat at the back of the barber shop, in between two old men reading newspapers. Her body looked the same, but, as he'd thought on the train, her face looked older, the shade under her eyes had deepened. Her hair was now dyed a bright red, and when she cut the back of the bloke's hair, she still bent low to do it, pushing her bum out towards the men waiting in chairs like she always had.

Kasha had shown no reaction to seeing him, but when she finished the haircut she was doing when he came in, she went out through a black curtain and into the back room. There were three customers waiting but the other girl had to do all the cuts. When it was time for Greg to get his done, he sat in the chair with his shoulders hunched. He could feel sweat creeping up his back as the girl shoved his head this way and that. At one point she stood right in front of him to check his fringe. But it wasn't like it could have been if Kasha had done it.

Before getting the train back he wandered around the town, eventually going in Greggs and getting a pie and a cup of tea. He sat on a bench outside the cathedral, looking out across the market square and with a clear sight of the barber shop. There were gulls and jackdaws on the paving stones around his feet, and he dropped bits of pie crust for them to squabble over. After an hour or so he got up and shook his head and shrugged and walked back down the hill to the train station.

His parents' tiny house was on a farm estate, and his

dad still worked on the farm. The rent on the house was low because of that, but it had single glazed windows and no insulation and the wind off the hills blew right through it. But, day and night, all year round his mum kept the coal fire going. It heated the house and the hot water and when the sun had been out all day, Greg's tiny bedroom got warm enough. But the rooms of the house that had been big enough before he left were now no longer big enough. Upstairs the two bedrooms were separated only by the tiny bathroom, and in that bathroom the bath was so small that Greg had to bend his knees to lie down in it.

On his first night back, he had heard screaming in the night. That first time he had jumped out of bed and looked out through his tiny window. In his mind he thought of a girl being raped. But he could see nothing from the window except the ghostly shapes and shadows of sheep lying down in the moonlit field. He returned to the warmth of his bed, and when his heart stopped beating so fast settled back to sleep. The next time he heard the screaming it sounded exactly the same and this made him think it had come from his own mind. He'd never had nightmares before, and he felt lucky that way. This screaming seemed to him that he was getting off lightly, and because it always sounded the same, he just got used to it.

There were two boys, Matthew and Christopher who lived in the house next door. Matthew had a mop of blonde hair while Christopher had dark, short hair and wore brown glasses. It was the summer holidays. Their mother, Lacey, was at her wits' end. One morning, as Greg was walking past their house with his rucksack on, she came to her garden gate. She had long black hair and though she looked tired she still seemed very beautiful to him. When Greg was a boy, he had watched the woman next door. Sometimes in summer she lay on a sun lounger in a bikini.

Are you going far? Lacey asked.

Just up to the lake.

Can I ask you a big favour? Can you take the boys with you?

Yeah, sure. It will be muddy up there though.

Oh, don't worry about that. Matthew! Christopher!

The boys came running into the garden.

Greg says he will take you up to the lake.

The boys got all excited and ran back to their house before coming back out again, running and trying to put on their shoes at the same time.

Have you got jackets? said Greg. Bring something waterproof. I don't think it is going to rain, but you never know.

Lacey went back for their jackets, thin waterproofs not really sufficient but better than nothing. Then she closed the garden gate behind them, heading straight back to the house and not turning around to see them walking up the road.

They took a right at the footpath sign and passed through the farm gate onto a track filled with highland cattle gathered around a feeder where hay spilled out onto the mud. Matthew and Christopher stood behind Greg, always keeping Greg between them and the cattle. The track took a route between a drystone wall and a canopy of trees and the three of them went along slipping and sliding.

My dad says he's getting me some wellies! shouted Matthew.

Well then, I want some too! said Christopher.

Greg looked down at his own boots all slick and brown with wet mud, and finally the path spread out onto a grassy hillside and they walked up that hillside and stood overlooking the lake. They might have been somewhere in Canada or Sweden maybe, it looked like a real wilderness with the lake and the surrounding pines. But a road ran along across the top of the moors behind, and anyone passing in a car could see them.

Great view from here, lads, said Greg. Not everyone gets to grow up in a place like this you know.

My dad says he's going to teach me how to drive the tractor! said Matthew.

You want to work on the farm then?

Yeah.

You going to do the same job as your dad?

Yeah, I am. I'm going to be a tractor driver and have my own wellies and everything!

What about you, Christopher?

I'm going to go and live in America.

Really?

Yes, the United States of America.

Oh, and what are you going to do in the United States of America?

I'm going to be a superhero.

A superhero?

Yes. Ant-Man!

Good for you, said Greg. Good for you.

From the lake they walked on past the ruins of an old farmstead where rabbits in their dozens hurtled and jumped and ran down warrens with their little white backsides in the air. Matthew told how his dad shot rabbits and how they ate rabbit stew all the time, and how his dad was going to show him how to shoot when he was old enough. Greg had done the same as a boy. He remembered once how he and his friend Robert had killed one and made a start on trying to skin it. But they didn't know how and Robert puked up at the sight of the spilling intestines.

In the middle of the moorland there was a fencepost with arrows pointing three ways. They took a right and jumped over a trickling burn and climbed to the top of another little hill, where they could see across to more rolling hillsides filled with pine plantations.

There's the train! shouted Christopher, the sunlight reflecting from his glasses.

They looked down into the valley and there it was, the blue train, the local, a train that was new back in the 60s but that was now old fashioned, comparatively slow. Just two carriages with the sunlight shining through and one or two heads in the windows. It made a lot of noise and after it passed Greg still felt like he had done as a boy. Who were those faces in the windows, where were they getting off, what were their lives? And when the train took its curve around the valley floor and the sound of it eventually faded, it felt like something significant, however brief, was over, and all would be silent until the next train came through.

Greg's dad was always out working. He could have returned home for lunch but preferred to stay in the Portakabin, tucked away in the corner of a great yard filled with old tractors and tractor parts next to a massive barn filled with hay bales. Greg wanted to see him and, as he had done many times as a boy, headed for the Portakabin with a piece of fruit for his dad.

Approaching the Portakabin, he looked in through the window. His dad was sitting there smoking a roll up, next to two of the other farm workers. The dog was on the floor. When Greg knocked on the door and walked in his dad made no expression at all, took the apple without any recognition or nostalgia. But when Greg didn't say anything and turned to walk back out, he got up and followed his son into the yard.

Come and help me move the sheep.

Okay, said Greg.

They walked together down the tree lined road to the field below the earthworks where the sheep were grazing, Alfie the border collie running on ahead of them. Greg watched as his dad started up the 4×4 and Alfie jumped on the back. It wasn't like when he was a boy, when it was all done on foot. And when Red the old border collie was still alive. Greg didn't know this new dog at all. His dad looked the same though, tall and slender and round shouldered, just older, and like his mum, the hair greyer than before.

After his dad had moved the sheep onto fresh grazing, he drove the 4×4 back down the hill, back to where Greg was standing.

Sit on the end, lad, he said to Greg. Greg jumped up and sat on the back of the 4×4 as his dad started rolling a cigarette. Still his dad didn't ask him anything.

Greg looked across the valley to the rolling hillsides on the other side of the river. Dad, you know something, I get nightmares.

Oh aye? he said, not looking up from his cigarette.

Well, not nightmares exactly. I just hear screaming.

Oh aye, he said again, scratching the grey growth of beard on his chin. How often is this, like?

Err ... well, now and again, not every week.

His dad looked around before finally making eye contact. Greg could see how red rimmed and bloodshot his dad's eyes were. At least it's not every night, son, he said.

Greg looked across to the field of sheep. Some of them were huddled in the shade of walls, others in the shadows of the tall trees that lined the road. High above, buzzards glided on thermals. Greg stepped off the 4×4 and his dad drove it back towards the yard. As the sound of the engine faded, Greg ran his hands through his hair and watched as two men came walking across the field towards him.

Barren Clough

D ON'T YOU LOVE the way that sunlight in spring makes everything stunning, when the grass is arrayed with sprays of light, birds' flight catches the colour, the stillness of budding trees is changed slightly by the evening breeze and the fresh air is filled with trills?

It was the coldest winter for thirty or forty years; a winter where snow covered the high hills almost constantly for three months from November and the council's JCB didn't get to grit the road until the day before the defrost, the day the village began to murmur with the mention of heads.

It was when the farmer went out into his fields after the thaw that he saw them. The road up out of the village had been thickened with snow and then that snow had iced over, and the same thing down in the village meant sprained wrists and ankles, and an old boy called Magic aggravating a hernia.

Jack lost his wife some years before, and sometimes you would see him in the tractor with his grandson on his knee as they drove up and over the hills. The farmyard held a high pole with a flag of St George at the top, and in its flapping or oblong shadow there was a pond, collected at the bottom of Barren Clough. It was a pit stop for geese flying between reservoirs.

Jack's black and white cows farted all winter so that when the wind blew in certain directions, you'd think the tin roof of the cow shed might blow off with the force of accumulated methane. In summer when he let them out, they wandered black and white across the hills, chewing their way across the skyline, eating the low slung branches off the blossoms in Barren Clough. Sometimes the same noises that came from the shed rang out across the moonlit hills as a strangulated plea that seemed to send a shudder through the leaves.

It was an evening by the pond as Jack tinkered with his tractor that he saw the moonlight shining on something unusual by the bottom of the Clough. Half in the flagpole's shadow, it floated like a sponge, sinking only slightly as the water's weight collected and slowly sucked it down.

Because of the pond and the sight of the others after the snow's thaw, Jack got out his shotgun and donned his deer-stalker cap and started roaming across the fields. On the other side of the hills the wind struck him as he squinted across to the trees. He looked down at the houses on the lane and thought of how most of his old friends had died quietly of old age, wondered at the new occupants he didn't know, the youngsters that pulled their faces in their cars when they had to wait as he drove down the lane with hay bales the same way he'd done for forty years.

As he looked down at the houses on the lane, Jack thought of his own youth, when he'd moved to the village. He'd got to know a couple of old boys in the pub and they played dominoes in the evening. George and Jim scoffed at the notion of Jack calling himself a local. Jack asked how you qualified and George told him to come back in twenty-five years, and when he did George was dying. Jack went into the pub and asked for his usual Guinness and the landlady came back with a double whisky from George.

Jack spent all his days on the farm, working harder and harder to get less and less for what he produced. So, the shotgun came out and he carried on searching every morning. One night he dreamt his washing line was filled with yellow spiders, bats flew back and forth in the sky and all his windows were covered by mosquitoes.

What Jack couldn't know at first was how it had been done. As a farmer he knew that the threat had been eliminated by many years of killing. He couldn't envisage that coming back, but after weeks and weeks of wandering, after talking to anyone in the village old enough to know what he was talking about, it came to him that maybe, just maybe, they were back. He started to listen as well as look and it was that that gave him confirmation as he lay in bed listening back to the tenor of his dreams.

In his youth Jack had seen them and wondered why they'd had to do it. And when he went out looking for them again and couldn't find them, all those years later, he started to have nightmares about his youth, his boyish clean-shaven face reappearing among collages, collages like those in the paintings of Hieronymus Bosch.

He knew not to frighten them off by making them aware of his presence, and he guessed he'd have to act fast before they moved away. He began to observe them from his vantage point in the conservatory, his binoculars trained on the skies above the cow shed and Barren Clough at the horizon line. Night after night he sat there looking at the changing colours of the sky, a sky sometimes white, sometimes blue, often a pervading grey, sometimes a sedentary fire, sometimes yellow, sometimes pink; all the time shining through the trees. And for a time, he couldn't see the patterns.

Eventually Jack saw them from the conservatory and grabbed his gun and deerstalker cap and set off out the back of the farm and straight up Barren Clough to the trees on the hillside. He felt the climb in his legs like he never used to, but annoyance and adrenalin hastened him higher until he got to a hiding place behind the trunk of an oak he'd seen rise over forty years.

The shotgun was ready and Jack lifted its weight higher but he had to be sure before starting to blast. One of them landed briefly in the branches of the oak and Jack shot upward and brought down great branches on top of himself.

After bringing down the branches it seemed to Jack that he'd missed his chance and the red skies went quiet for a while. But inexplicably, tauntingly, they came back in numbers, the red winter sky filled with spiralling blackness and the silences of the hills gone to their gliding, accumulated call.

Jack blasted at the sky, shell after shell, the shotgun ramming his shoulder in the cannonade. He stood there in the growing red, the strength draining from his arms, and then the blackness turned thicker before turning in a wind gust to white. The snow came down heavier and heavier, and though a part of his mind kept telling him to turn around, a stronger, louder part told him that this was something that needed doing now, and so he kept blasting into the snowfall, blasting until the snow stopped and the sky cleared and all was covered by stars.

The flight of ravens covers the sky in glory. You don't see them because the years of persecution are ingrained. And in those bygone days there were reasons above and beyond deeper concerns like the flight of birds. But now, if you are lucky, maybe a child on an old man's knee on a tractor, you might see them, their wingspan shadowing counties, their flight from hilltop to hilltop faster than any high speed train you might imagine, and much quieter, infinitely more elegant than any invention. And if you get close enough you can hear the vastness of that wingspan as a heavy brush on the sky, and you will know you have seen it and heard it because you will feel it deep down inside yourself, know that the blackness will never go to grey, know what is beyond all government control, and you yourself will fly beyond bullets into the limitless vistas of the sky.

Ceum na Caillich

THEY LEFT THE camper van in the car park, intent on a horseshoe walk that would take them up the mountain. Following the burn along a distinct path they looked at the glistening and shining waterfalls that ran down past them and collected in deep pools.

Emerging through a pine plantation they saw the skyline and the dress circle ridge along which Emma had planned they would walk; a dress circle ridge leading to The Witch's Step. They crossed the burn higher up and began a tough ascent through cotton grass and bracken and heather. The path, distinct on the other side of the burn, eroded now into a loop of hard stones before fading into a flattening of the cotton grass. White butterflies flew all around them.

Suze stopped, breathing heavily, disheartened, her heart never having been in the walk in the first place. Emma had always walked. Suze knew it. And she knew that she had to show some enthusiasm. Emma had taken her to all of the places she'd walked before. They'd never gone anywhere new. Suze had always said to Emma how she wanted to go to the west of Ireland and meet her relatives there.

But they always went back to Emma's beloved Scotland.

Come on, said Emma, brushing away midges. You'll have it dark. You wanted to do these kinds of walks so come on, let's get on with it. It'll be easier once we get up there.

I just need to sit down for a minute, said Suze, easing herself down onto a slanted rock. Emma stood above her, smilingly competitive, gazing up at the ridge in the sky she knew to be the promontory of stunning views.

When Suze stood up, Emma at once began marching off ahead of her again, following the contours of the land now that the path seemed to have vanished, bearing right and then swinging left to make a more gradual ascent. She loved how these mountain trails always seemed to take the most intelligent course, the routes of crofters before the clearances. When she was inexperienced, she had made short cuts, taking straight lines for the summit, making her ascents much quicker and considerably more arduous. By now she'd mellowed a little, and when she remembered she made a conscious choice to slow down, to enjoy being on the mountain, to look around at the broadening vista or closer at the shifting white of the cotton grass. But she didn't look back to see where Suze was and Suze cursed her out of earshot.

It was clear how the Witch's Step got its name. Where the ridge rolled along gently across the summit in a series of benevolent tors, at the notorious step the summit slipped starkly downwards, cutting a slanted and treacherous V into the mountain.

Suze was too tired to have realized their prospective route, and Emma hadn't told her. Emma remembered when she'd done this walk previously, the fear she'd felt that first time so many years before, on her own, when the sun had been blazing, the day she'd been ravaged by horseflies. She'd stayed in the village and done a walk around the headland to a deserted white cottage. There she'd sat down in hot sunshine and looked out at the haze above the water. The water blurred with the sky. A seal was basking on a rock and the coastline was completely silent. The ghostly reflections of white yachts floated motionlessly on the flat water. A man in a kayak passed as though slowly flying. And time and again Emma was bitten by horseflies.

It was these memories that made Emma doubt herself below the Witch's Step. She thought it a sly joke that experience had made her feel more vulnerable rather than more confident. She had sprung down the descent without problems that last time. The weather had been sunny then. She was older now and Suze was older than she was. Emma was surprised by the way she herself was sweating and breathing heavily.

As they sat apart, Emma gulping their water, Suze took in the view down towards the sea loch. Grey clouds blew in as Suze remembered when they'd stayed there, and how there were no facilities except a little sandwich shop and a butcher, and how she missed the Co-Op. She remembered how, on a bright sunny day, they'd walked along the road to the tiny ferry port.

As she nibbled at her oatcakes, Suze could see the tiny ferry crossing the dark waters of the sound. On that day previously, Emma had insisted they go back to the hotel, and with the hot sun and the views outside they sat in the little lounge bar. Emma had ordered white bait for them. Suze left half of it and sat there in the shaded surrounds, thinking of the ferry crossing, and the sun outside, and the ruins of the castle, and how it seemed they always did what Emma wanted them to do. In the corrie, groups of red deer, some half hidden by bracken, looked directly across at them, ears raised, before moving away and looking back again. One of them made a gentle grunt in their direction.

The distance of the walk was just over six miles, with about three thousand feet of total ascent. And it was about halfway through that Suze thought it would have been wise for them to turn back. With dark clouds gathering, they were already too tired. But after a short rest they continued a little further upwards and the route flattened out to a clearly marked ridge walk. For Emma these ridges were the best kind of walking. The high ground reached, she was able to stroll and look around for ravens and eagles. Suze welcomed the respite too, for a forgotten moment even seeming to enjoy the adventure of it, an adventure she didn't know the half of yet. In the silences of the summit walk Suze heard the beguiling croak of a couple of ravens, high overhead. It wasn't their loud calling, it was a gentle communication between the two birds, and it sounded intimate, as though they held the privacy of the sky.

Emma and Suze put on their jackets in preparation for what seemed the inevitable rain, and when it came it lashed them in a rushing wind, a wind Emma hoped would mean the rain passed over them quickly. It didn't. As the rain came the wind dropped again, and a view she'd been expecting of another mountain was lost behind the black drift of the clouds. The granite tors around them slickened in the wet and Emma abandoned any plan to climb to the summit. Now was the time to keep as close to the path as they could. And still they had yet to reach the Witch's Step.

When they reached the jagged descent, Emma instructed Suze to follow her exact route. Suze looked down into the chasm and couldn't believe she'd take them on a walk as dangerous as this, worse that she wouldn't tell her about it first. It was typical of her selfishness. She couldn't go all the way back. In her fatigue she almost didn't care if she fell. She had been stumbling from tiredness across the edges of the easy ridge path, and she watched as Emma inched her way down, her hands grabbing the granite before she sat on her backside, seemingly about to slide. Suze watched Emma's progress from above and looked beyond her to the gully where they'd be safe. Emma's legs were fatigued, and when her heel slipped, Suze watched. Her head glanced off a granite outcrop. Then she seemed to stop a moment before falling more rapidly. In the silence broken only by the rain, Suze heard Emma land in the gully some thirty feet below.

Suze stopped still for a moment, her heart racing, and immediately saw how Emma should have descended; there was a thin trail between rocks that clearly showed a safer way. She gripped the wet granite in her hands as she went down, hugged it in parts so that the sharp rock ripped at her jacket and ragged at her fingers.

In the gully she grabbed wet granite and steadied her shaking legs, took a deep breath and then walked over to Emma. Her head was covered in blood and she was unconscious. Suze took off her coat and covered the crumpled body. She searched the numbers in her mobile and tried calling mountain rescue but there was no reception. She reached into Emma's pockets for the keys to the camper van and then covered her again with her coat. She could see through the rain towards a path off to the left leading down the gully, and then a path leading off from that to the right, around the base of the Witch's Step. She checked the mobile but still there was no reception.

Suze followed the clear path. There was a ray of sunlight through the shifting clouds and for a moment the granite on the footpath sparkled. Suze looked across to the grey immensity of the sound that seemed joined to the grey waves of cloud in the sky. There was a tiny white yacht alone out there.

Suze kept descending on a very steep path that disappeared into heather and thistle and bracken and thorns, all the time stopping to check her phone. Finally, she saw the white camper van, tiny in the parking area. There were no other cars and she looked at her mobile phone again. Still there was no reception. Shivering with adrenaline and cold she continued towards the van.

Few cars passed along the long tarmac road that ran down the hill. Suze struggled through a group of trees near the valley floor and heard a raven in the rain. She struggled lower and lower, continually slipping onto her backside, before she ploughed through a stretch of heather and slicked bracken and thorns and finally stepped onto the tarmac.

As Suze sat in the camper van she started to scratch at her hands, her neck and the small of her back. Then she started to scratch at her face. She looked back into the van with its kitchen unit and the little fridge, and the couch that folded out into a bed, and there were midges everywhere.

She looked at the phone and still there was no reception. With all the windows open and the heater blasting, she started the camper van and pulled out of the parking area, heading south. She reached the hotel and called the mountain rescue from the landline in the lobby. They told her to stay where she was. She watched through the rain lashed windows as the waves washed ashore. A little old lady offered tea to calm her nerves. She drank it, was warmed by the gesture and the liquid even as she burned her tongue. The rain crashed against the windows. Suze looked at the sky, heard the rumble. She ran outside into the rain and looked up and saw the yellow mountain rescue helicopter disappearing and reappearing among the clouds. She waved at it, pointed stupidly toward the hills. Cyclists passed in procession along the coastal road, oblivious to everything but the rain.

The old lady in the hotel was talking to a barmaid. When Suze looked towards them, they looked away. The old lady came back with some cheese and told Suze to eat. Suze laughed at the sight of the cheese on the plate. She got back in the van and drove back to the car park. All the way back she tried to look up for the helicopter and more than once nearly knocked over a cyclist. She braked to a halt on the gravel of the car park and got out of the van. There were no cars on the road, just cyclists labouring up the hill. The rain had stopped but the Sannox Burn roared under the bridge. She was bitten on her hand by a mosquito. An eagle floated above the ridge line. Suze couldn't hear or see the helicopter. Still there was no reception on her phone. She stood in the car park as the roaring of the burn grew louder. There was an information board showing a map and detailing wildlife and flora and fauna. She kicked at it then looked at the van. She'd left the driver's door open. The keys were swinging from the ignition.

She got back in the van. She passed the bunkhouse where they'd stayed on a previous visit. She looked at the picnic tables under the wet parasols that looked out across the sound, remembering another stupid argument there. The scenic places of Scotland were just venues for their bickering, and Emma had never respected her.

Driving on she saw the stone seal on a rock that fools everyone on their first visit. The seal that, even when the waves lash over it stays fixed in the same place, unlike the real seals that slip easily off their rocks as the tide comes in. Further out, she saw the approach of the ferry.

She took her hands off the wheel to scratch at them, swerving a little on the narrow coast road. She scratched at her neck and face as she passed another castle, almost hitting a cyclist. She drove further around the bay to the car park at the ferry port. She went into the boarding area, showing her return ticket to a man in a little yellow cabin.

In the claustrophobic parking area in the hull of the boat she sat there as others pulled up beside and behind her. She stayed still as the ferry started its crossing, sitting in the camper van Emma had bought for them. As she stared through the window at the car in front, alarms started going off all around her.

A Place Like This

PULLING THE DOOR closed behind her, she walks past the car and beyond the drive, continuing through the village until she reaches the first footpath sign. She climbs over the stile and immediately feels in a different place. Walking through the village she'd felt the eyes of the locals, imagined their mutterings, perceived the twitching of the curtains. Now she's up above the village and climbing gradually higher into the hills she feels the noose from around her neck loosening, easing off, if never actually being removed.

Looking down at the mud on the path she can see the patterned prints of pheasants, further on, rabbits start spiralling across the grass, dead ones among them festering and fly blown, trickles of frozen red on the solid green. There's a sheep's rotting carcass, the eyes gone where the crows got at them, flapping wool, yards away more wool, wind-blown and caught in the crannies of a drystone wall.

She passes the desolate, abandoned farmhouse, looks inside at the fireplace, imagines the views from inside. Thinks of the family that once lived there in a time when you could make a living in a place like this.

This morning she had almost switched the computer on, logged onto the company intranet, thought to start something, something easy, to begin the long catch up necessitated by her absence. But the sunlight above the elms dictated otherwise, she'd felt that urge, that instinct, to get out of the lovely house no amount of interior design could bring life to, and at the breakfast table, as the frost in the fields began to recede in the warmth of the sunlight, and the first birds in her sight line crossed the window in languid wing strokes above a landscape that had seemed the fulfilment of a dream, she decided to put on her boots.

At lunchtime, among the consoling cotton grass, she can hear the pheasants, and if she listens carefully, the pheasant chicks that will grow and get shot for sport. She sees none of the birds that occasionally predate the pheasants, for the buzzards have been poisoned and there are no hen harriers anymore. She hears the call of the curlew, and that call returned, a spectral echo that reaches through the absences of the moorland. Later, the curlews become aware of her again and circle in broadening arcs, their throaty whistles receding.

She thinks of work, the intranet login, that intranet login that will lead her to his emails, and his name over and over in the list on the left, and she will click on them and reply to them, and they will be caged in banality, in appropriateness, for fear of violating the acceptable use policy, and they will keep up this charade, and in every waking moment she will be hurt by his words. Bastard underling. How did she let this happen to herself? Clown on a bike, smiling up at her window like he was something to her. And the brazen smiles of the acquaintances at work, how she hated them.

She reaches a series of gritstone boulders strewn together across the high reaches of the landscape, above the valley leading down to the pubs, the hotel, the camp site and the train station. These are a series of big stones jutting from the landscape, shaped by the elements, some more distinctly than others, and given names like the Mushroom, the Salt Cellar, the Kissing Stones and the Stool. These are boulders beloved of climbers, though there is no obvious climbing going on today. The routes up the rocks have names like Pinky Ponk and Ninky Nonk, Wide Eyes Shut and Novel Adaptation. But they are a bit too small for proper bouldering, like she did that time in France. It was different there. The sun made the rocks warm, and if you came off you landed in sand. She remembers one boulder in Fontainebleau, how she couldn't even get onto it, couldn't make a start. He put his thumb on the tiniest of ledges, and twisted his whole body around on it, so it seemed all his weight was held by a pivoting thumb. He smiled as he did it, having watched her struggle.

She takes off her woolly hat, and her long hair is blown back by the wind. Soon the cold hurts her forehead, but she keeps the hat off, likes the sting, remembers to feel the sting. She remembers also the time they came together, that time of high summer, midweek, less people jabbering.

She recalls how they sat there, looking along the ridge-line, and then how she sat on him, her senses spiralling, and then heard at last the tiny whistling, and looked up to see fleeting squadrons of them, all the swifts in the world silhouetted on the clean blue sky, causing her to squint towards the sun. And she sits there now, waiting for the swifts or that feeling from the time of the swifts, not knowing that the swifts will never return for her here at this time or at any other time, because there are no swifts left for her anymore, just swallows mistaken for swifts by those who know nothing of birds.

She unscrews her flask. The sun glints on its tannin-stained interior. She pours the glinting tea into a blue plastic cup, takes sandwiches out of a blue lidded lunch box. Eats the cheese sandwiches, bites into an apple, looks towards the route she will take back, along the cliff edge to see the ravens, through the low lying fields where the lapwings burble and sparkle and plummet and rise, back into the village where the jackdaws line the telegraph wires or huddle around the warm surrounds of chimneys above greasy slates, back into the house, where she will take off her boots, hang her coat and hat above the radiator in the hallway, feel her face glowing from the weather, make more tea, sit with it at the kitchen table watching through the window, peering into the dusk for dunnocks and robins and blackbirds.

In the last field before the village, she treads across the tussocks of grass, her mind searching into the future. She is old now. A kid would look at her as though she were old anyway. There are wisps of grey hair on her cheeks. There was an advert on the telly for something that could get rid of it. There was another advert filled with happy families, so many adverts filled with happy families. She is thinking of the future as she treads on the egg. She looks down and sees the grey container split, the corpse of the lapwing chick splayed out, and only then does she hear the lapwings in the air.

Year after year, on Sundays after church bells and walking, she sits down to the TV and watches the same programme charting the decline of our bird populations, and she pays more and more in her subscription to the RSPB, but year on year she hears about the disappearing swifts and there's nothing to be done.

One evening, she's in the garden and looks up at the roof of her house. Under the guttering, in a shaded nook, she sees house martins clinging without effort to the brickwork, darting in and out of a nest that has been there the whole time.

A voice comes over the fence. Lovely, aren't they?

I've never seen them, she says.

You must be able to hear them?

Er . . .

I'm assuming that's above your bedroom, right?

Is it?

Logical, isn't it? My house is laid out the same, I'd imagine.

Sorry, what's your name?

Phil.

Hi, Phil.

I didn't get your name.

Oh sorry, my phone is ringing, she says, rushing back into the house where the signal is usually weaker. She answers the call. The voice is crackly. It has an Indian accent. Life Insurance cover. She knows before he speaks. Has she considered it? No, she says, she is not interested. What would be the point?

She starts going into town on Saturdays, catching the train to where the line ends and walking down the hill to the shops. They are refurbishing the spa, with its curved sweep of building, and there's the stone monument around what purports to be the original spring, where people can drink for free rather than going over the road to the shop where they sell it in plastic bottles.

She likes the town, with its outdoor shops selling budget gear that would be no use in any real extremes, and its charity shops filled with faded dresses, hats, mirrors and musty books. She goes in a café that has been open for over a hundred years, according to the signage, and sells all different kinds of tea, and she sits there at a tiny corner table by the window overlooking the main street, sips her loose-leaf tea from its ornate pot and watches the world pass by. There are so many people walking dogs here. There are dogs everywhere. There's that thing where strangers will bond over dogs, an old man will reach in his pocket for dog treats when he doesn't even have a dog with him, will feed those dog treats to a stranger's dog, and they will talk about the dog and smile and laugh, talk about old dogs they've had, and she will know of none of that because she hates dogs, was bitten on the hand by one when she was seven. It wasn't a deep bite, more of a nip, but the unpredictable nature of it still makes her wary.

She goes into the park. There's a model train carrying families around on winding rails. There's the picture postcard stretches of river, the manufactured landscapes of gentility that contrast so starkly with the barren splendour of the wind-racked moors high above them, moors that she knows will still be wind-racked on this day of sunshine, when it is nice enough for ice cream, and the park is full up, and a brass band plays on the bandstand.

She sits on a bench, licks her ice cream, listens to the music. She's always loved this sound, she realizes, but has never followed up on it, has never been to watch brass bands before, though she has a vague memory of watching a film. They are playing a song she knows. She has heard of colliery bands, but never bought any of the music, and though she tries to discount it the warmth of it touches her, and she's glad the bands still play, though there are no collieries anymore.

Culverts

THE PUB IS on a long road between two counties, a twisting tarmac route beloved of motorcyclists with a death wish.

If you had a telly we could watch, Chris says.

I'm not getting a telly. And anyway, we are right here, why do you need to see it on TV?

I was watching it before. They was interviewing Lucy.

Oh right. It's going to affect business down in the town that's for sure.

That's what she was on about.

I'm not leaving, whatever happens.

You'll be fine up here.

They still trying to get you to leave?

Yep. Police are getting a bit nasty now. But like I said they're just covering their own arses.

Health and safety.

That's what it is, I know we go on about it but that's what it is. Anyway, if it goes my house will be gone.

Stay here.

That's what I'm doing. And if I'm at home and I hear them sirens going I won't be getting out of town. I haven't got a car anyway. They just assume we've all got cars.

Come up here.

That's what I was going to say, I'll just come up here and we can see it out from here. And then when they say it was a false alarm I'll just be sitting where I would have been anyway.

It won't come to that.

No. If anything I quite like it with all the roads closed. You can hear all the birds now. It's pretty amazing.

Roads will open again soon. Bad for business. All the lorries need to get where they're going. For the quarries and that.

Just then, Lucy comes in. I'll have a Merlot, large, she says.

You alright, Lucy?

Do I look alright, Chris?

Is it the choppers?

Course it is, I've been fucking closed a week now. How am I going to survive this shit?

It makes a change for them to have someone different to talk to. You'd get these hikers coming in after a long day on the hills, sunburn on their noses or the back of their necks, and they'd go redder after one pint, and sometimes they'd stay for three or four before getting on the train back home.

Fucking Prime Minister comes in my shop and he's wanting a bacon butty, she says, and I told him we haven't got any power and anyway I didn't know he was coming, did I? All these helicopters all over the place, I didn't know there was another one bringing him, did I? I wouldn't mind but I never voted for him in the first place and he comes in the shop and he knows the cameras are on him and he comes out with all this shit and then five minutes later, he's gone.

She glugs from the Merlot, doesn't lick the wine off her lip. It sits there like a moustache as she goes on. I've come here. I've left him with the kids. He's getting on my tits. He can't get out to work, can he? Roads closed, trains closed, it's doing my head in.

You've come to the right place, says Gary.

Fill me up, she says, and Gary does so, and they are big wine glasses, and soon enough Lucy begins to slow down a bit. Drinkers are down on themselves and Chris likes that. He remembers back to when she'd first worked behind the bar.

You've been sitting there for years, she says.

Yep.

Why?

Why not?

If it's not broken don't change it, right?

That's one way to put it.

That's why saddo's like you never change.

Better the devil you know.

Just fucking words, Chris, they're just fucking words, aren't they? I mean, look at you, you just come here every day and that's it. No ambition.

Yep.

How can you do that?

Easy.

You've got no responsibilities either, have you? Like me, I've got him and the kids, and, oh, don't let me forget, I've got to go back there soon.

I'll get you one more, Chris says.

No responsibilities. You are free as a bird and free to fly around like a bird.

Kind of.

How come you've never had kids?

Just haven't. Not that I know of anyway, he says, smiling.

That's not a nice thing to say, Chris, but I'll let you off since you've got me a drink.

Never wanted them. To be honest, I hate kids.

No need for that. I bet he's a jaffa, eh, Gary?

A what?

A jaffa, fires blanks.

Maybe I am, so what?

You're a jaffa.

Has its advantages. Saves on johnnies.

Don't start being a dick now, Chris.

I'm not, anyway, it's time for me to head back.

Will you walk me down the hill?

No, sorry, he says, walking off, leaving her at the bar.

The storms forecast for that night never come and by lunchtime next day it still hasn't rained. It is weird though. Without going into climate change and everything, the rain does seem to come down harder. It has always rained a lot, seems to rain almost every day and even more so in summer than winter, but those recent rains have come down so hard, so fast, that the village can't cope, and the council hasn't ever properly sorted the culverts even after last time, and now this latest stuff up at the reservoir, a reservoir that is apparently two hundred years old, this latest stuff means that at any moment, according to the authorities, the dam could burst and flood the whole village.

 ❦

Chris walks up the hill again and back into the pub. Lucy is sitting on his stool.

You're late, Christopher, she says.

Am I?

And where the fuck did you go the other night, Christopher?

Went home at my normal time.

Fucking hell, Gary, what's he like?

Gary just shakes his head.

What are you doing back in here anyway? Chris asks her.

Don't ask silly questions, Christopher. Buy me a drink.

I'll buy you a drink if you stop calling me Christopher and let me sit on my own stool.

Creature of habit, Chris, creature of habit. That's the problem with people like you.

He sits on his stool and Lucy sits on the one next to him.

Merlot?

You remembered, Chris, she says, sarcastically.

Yeah, he responds.

He sits in silence as she talks. She speaks of her frustrations, how the threat of the dam bursting is destroying her business, and how, if it goes on for much longer, she'll have to lay off staff. She wonders why the dam is two hundred years old, why it hasn't been replaced, or at least checked more often, how it has reached such a breaking point.

And in the end, she comes back to the choppers, how they stop her sleeping, how all their efforts at dropping bags of concrete into the bit of the dam that is broken are probably about as much use as a chocolate fireguard.

She's had three wines to his two pints, tells him she needs to talk outside. He follows her out and she tugs at his shirt, stares at him a bit glassy eyed. They walk past the back of the pub and up to the cricket ground.

He tries the patio doors for a laugh, and they are open. They go in the pavilion and get on a couch in one of the changing rooms. He lifts her legs up, so they are resting on his shoulders, and goes deep into her. He looks down as she puffs her cheeks out. He keeps going, but then it's finished and she doesn't even look at his face.

Oh my god, she says. That was stupid, I can't believe what you've just done, she says.

What?

What's wrong with me? It's these fucking helicopters. I haven't slept for weeks.

We're probably on a drone camera.

Oh, don't fucking make jokes.

Be on YouTube now.

Fucking joke to you this, isn't it?

They'd first got together five years before. Communicated via Messenger, started meeting in secret places. The best time had been at this hotel outside Chester. Nobody knew them and they walked around like a couple. They'd jumped on the bed as soon as they got in the room, then they went to the spa, had a swim, sat in the jacuzzi together. Before dinner they were at it again, and at dinner he had pork belly with creamy mash and she had duck and chips, and for dessert he had a brownie with a compote of cherries and she had the sticky toffee pudding. They went back there three times in total, but it was never as good as the first time.

He'd see her around the village, sometimes go in the shop for a cake or a pie or something but it was always awkward. On seeing him she'd head back into the kitchen. He thought about her at night and kept messaging her but she got nervous and ended up blocking him.

⁂

An hour or so later a policeman comes in. He is sitting on Chris's stool when Chris comes back from the toilet.

Hello, what are you looking so guilty about, fella?

I'm not.

I'm just kidding, fella. We are just informing people to be careful about leaving their property. Do you have anyone at home now?

No.

Well that means your property is unguarded, fella. Most people complied with our orders and evacuated, but we don't have eyes everywhere. Anyway, the point is, there's a risk of burglary. We've had reports of looting. A pub in the village has had its back doors kicked in, and we've had reports of other incidents.

I've got nothing worth robbing.

That's not the attitude, fella.

Sorry.

You might have seen we have the drones operating, well that is nothing to be alarmed about, that is for your own security.

Okay thanks.

Just something to keep in mind.

Okay.

And if that dam goes, like you have been told many times, everyone left in the village is going to die.

There's no need for that. We're fine up here, says Gary.

That's as maybe. I'm not able to say. Like I say, lock up your property and leave the village, that remains our advice.

Okey dokey, says Gary. The usual, Chris?

Yep.

The policeman makes his way out, and the pub returns to silence, save for the sound of the choppers. It is late afternoon when Gary finally asks about Lucy.

She wanted a chat in private, Chris says.

Oh yeah?

She's stressed out, but I think she'll be fine.

Ah, women.

What do you mean?

They remain a mystery to me, a beautiful enigma.

God, you talk some bollocks, Gary.

None of my business, Chris, I just clean the glasses and pull the pints.

You've never been married then?

No.

Why's that?

It's not a big deal. I've known women. Plenty of women.

It had been easy when he was a young landlord, he had

the run of the barmaids. And when they left, as they inevitably did, there were always other ones turning up, looking for work.

The thing is, Gary, you don't sound like you know anything about women. You put them on a pedestal.

In my experience, women like that.

The sound of the choppers seems to get louder, come nearer, before finally moving away again.

I don't understand women, they have mood swings and that, they are more emotional, says Gary.

Bollocks.

Time of the month and that?

Well, whatever. Look, most people are arseholes, and some aren't, and the good ones, well, men or women, you try and stay friends with them, stay loyal to them, but in the end, they all just fuck you over.

But I've never seen you with a woman, Chris. You're always on your own.

And I've never seen you with a woman either, Gary.

But we've both known women.

Yes, we've both known women, but you don't *know* women.

At least I admit it.

Look, the thing is, I don't need women in my life anymore. And that's the thing, because I'm not interested, they keep turning up. I've had enough of it, trying to save people from themselves, trying to change people, trying to accept people as they are, going with the flow, trying to change myself. I've tried to live up to what women thought I was, and it's all bollocks. I'm old enough now not to give a fuck. The best relationship I had there was none of that, everything was easy, but I just fucked it up that's all, I was too young, didn't have the experience. That was my chance, and that was years ago now, over ten years ago, and there have been plenty of lovely women since then, women who have been through all that emotional shit and who just wanted a laugh, a bit of fun, and I'm over her, I'm over it all and I'm happy in my own company again, like I was when I was a kid, all those years ago before anything had ever happened to me. It's water under the bridge. I've always been happy in my own company. I don't get lonely, I'm not a needy person, one of them emotional leeches. A few beers and a view of the hills, that's me.

Come on, what's really going on with Lucy?

Are you even fucking listening to me? There's nothing to say. I'll have another.

No problem.

Cheers, he says.

※

It is surreal when the sirens get started, and the voices from the choppers get louder and louder. It sounds like the end of the world or something. Then for a few minutes it gets really quiet again and they can hear the birds.

Lucy has closed the shop early, gone for a drive, and is sitting in the car on the high moorland road above the reservoir. If it wasn't for the kids, she thinks, just before the sound of sirens.

They're all down there in the valley, in their beautiful house. She starts the car, heads down the hill, but already the road is sealed off. The police won't let her through, she's had plenty of warnings. She turns the car, speeds back up the hill, drives fast around a bend on the high moorland road, doesn't see the motorbike.

Needle in a Haystack

B ACK IN THE day there was this weird bookshop on an industrial estate next to a carpet shop and a mechanics, and though there were loads of signs most people had no idea it was there. It started in one industrial unit, but the owner, Osborne, owned the land, so, when the business expanded, he brought in shipping containers and filled them up with books. They were perfect for keeping out the rain and damp and you just padlocked them at night. The shop was near the motorway and the airport, and there was an airport parking place just around the corner, but it was a rip off.

The manager, Lee, was a local lad through and through. He had a wispy beard and a greasy ponytail and wore a leather fishing hat with a little City pin badge on. In winter he wore his walking gear: a green Regatta fleece and Karrimor walking boots, and in autumn used that walking gear on camping trips to the Llyn Peninsula.

Warren had gone to school with one of Osborne's sons from his second marriage and had been working part time in the shop, as a favour, for about five years. He'd been left a load of money and didn't really have to work and spent most of the rest of his time cycling around Cheshire on a three grand road bike.

Recycling Ray was in his sixties and had never been married. He wore silver rimmed glasses, had grey hair, lived alone, and drove around in a rusting yellow Mercedes van. He always wanted a chat in the shop and could tell you directions to virtually anywhere, in minute detail. He did a lot of work for little financial return. He went to all sorts of places, charity shops, car boot sales. He was the kind of endearing geek that you still felt had someone out there for him. The trouble with Ray was that he never seemed to listen to what anybody else said. There were a lot of people who came in that were a bit like that. They were on broadcast, not receive and another one of these was the Rubaiyat Man.

The Rubaiyat Man was rough round the edges and turned up in his white van with the name of the electrician firm on the side. Every time he came in he was looking for different versions of the *Rubaiyat of Ober Khayyam*. He'd recite it to anyone and everyone. He said that one day, in his forties, after a profound psychedelic experience during which he'd talked to God, he'd suddenly been able to remember all the poetry he'd learned by rote in school, Tennyson and all that. But his favourite was the Rubaiyat, though it was the earlier translations by Fitzgerald that he liked most, not the more recent ones. The old ones were more musical, had better rhymes. Lee once asked him what he thought the poem was about and Rubaiyat Man said fuck knows. He was into all sorts of stuff. He'd come in and talk about conspiracy theories, order books by Velikovsky and David Icke.

Virginia lived near the old Empire cinema that was now the Jehovah's Witness Hall, and she bobbed in whenever she felt like it. She didn't do computers and got eighty quid a week to put the books on the shelves, get in supplies for the kitchen, and generally keep the place tidy, which mainly involved going around with a Ewbank and cleaning the carpet tiles. In winter she came in wearing her husband's old fleece and a United bobble hat. She did the most physical work of anyone in the shop. Though she was in her seventies she was strong. For years she'd been a bodybuilder, entering competitions, and still went to the gym at least once a week.

&

One Wednesday afternoon a man stormed into the shop and looked like he was ready to wreck the place. He was a big bloke, had teeth missing, was dead pale. Bloodshot eyes stared out of his face.

Did you get some encyclopaedias in a bit back?

We get stuff in all the time, mate, said Lee.

Don't be funny. I know, but these encyclopaedias, very distinctive. Some weren't encyclopaedias, they were about the Roman Empire?

We get loads of that stuff in. But not recently, not as I recall. I can show you the ones we've got. Do you want them back or something?

The man didn't respond, but Lee took him over to a load of books blocking the fire escape. Those aren't them, we've had them ages, said Lee.

No, mate, no, but that's kind of what they looked like.

Look, what it is, and I'm not accusing anyone here, but what it is, is that my old fella is in hospital, not got long, being honest, and my mum thought she'd have a tidy of the house, make it nicer for him when he got back. So, she got rid of a load of books. Now I don't know why she thought getting rid of his books would make him feel better, I really don't, she's not been herself since he went in, none of us have. But anyway, she took some to the charity shop and some to bookshops, and she said she came in the one near the motorway, which I'm guessing is this one. It would have been about three months ago.

And why—

—Why what? Oh well, like I say, and I'm not accusing anyone, but there was an envelope in one of the books. And my old fella can't remember which one it was, just said it was in one of the big hardbacks at the top of the stairs, on the landing.

Anything we find in the books we put to one side, over here, said Lee, walking over to a shelf behind the counter which had all sorts of odds and sods on it: U.S. airline tickets from the mid-nineties, hand written notes, little black and white photographs.

I can't see any envelopes here, said Lee. Like I say, if anyone had seen it, it would be on here.

Okay, okay, well, like I say, I'm not accusing anyone. So, it would be a load of hardbacks about three months ago.

Yes, well, we get things in all the time, that's the problem, and we don't keep a record of it on the system either. But I'm in here most days, and I don't remember anything like that. What does your mum look like?

Well she's just an old lady.

So, she put all these heavy books in the car by herself?

What do you mean? Oh, yeah, she's hard as nails.

But she doesn't remember?

No, she says she doesn't, anyway. I don't want to accuse her either. I just want to find the books. Okay, look, my old fella said he made a little cut in the top of the spine with a knife, so he knew which one it was. You seen anything like that?

I'm sorry, mate, I don't remember. And I guess I would remember something like that. I can ask everyone else who works here.

Okay.

Do you want to leave us your number?

Okay, yeah, I will do, I was going to suggest that. Mobile is better, yeah, I will get you my mobile, he said, digging it out of his jeans pocket.

Okay, well, we'll call you then, if anything comes up. But I'm being honest, mate, it's a bit like looking for a needle in a haystack.

Okay. I'm going round the charity shops and a few other places, but like I said, she mentioned the place near the motorway, which is why I came here first.

Okay, well, we will definitely call you if anyone remembers anything.

Okay, thanks. I'm not accusing any of you that work here. Don't get me wrong.

No, it's fine. I mean, do you want to say what was in the envelope?

If anyone's seen the envelope, they'll know what's in it, believe me.

֍

Lee didn't say anything at the time, but he knew the lad by name. He was a Walsh, from one of the old gangs in the city, and his dad was Terry Walsh, who'd spent most of his time in prison over the years. Next time Osborne came in, Lee had to tell him about it, and Osborne wasn't happy.

The bloody Walshes! They were the bastards torched this place, one of his lads it was, did a year or so for it, nothing, but yeah, was them, stuffed rags through the letterbox! And now this cheeky sod is coming in asking about an envelope? Tell you what, if anyone has seen this envelope just keep it!

So, you haven't seen any envelope?

No, I haven't seen any bloody envelope!

I've asked Warren and Virginia, and they don't know anything about it. My gut feeling is that I don't think the books even came here, they probably went to a charity shop or something.

If anyone finds it, tell them to come straight to me, then we'll deal with the bloody Walshes.

֍

Tommy Walsh had long lived in the shadow of his father; years spent preparing for him to go to prison or preparing for him to come out, always the anti-climax of the coming out, when their quiet little house, only occasionally interrupted by new uncles, was filled again by his dad's elephant-in-the-room presence. Tommy always had to put up with the giggles of his mum that first night back, and the reduction in his standing within the house after that, until inevitably his dad ended up going back in and Tommy was the breadwinner again.

The Walshes had come from Ireland to work on the fairgrounds. There's the motorway barrelling through there now, but at one time, just down from the old Tatton Arms, where people used to come to watch boat races, there was a fairground down by the river. When the fairground closed some of the people working there stayed behind and there's a residential caravan park there now, beside the motorway, under the pylons.

Terry had moved them into a council house but they still kept the caravan in the front yard, taking a bit of fence off to fit it in, the caravan blocking all light into the front room.

Tommy's mum told him she thought Terry preferred it inside. Then the illness came, and he was in the prison hospital, and Tommy knew he wasn't ever coming out.

When his mum told him about the books and he passed it on to Terry, Terry's face turned red and he called her all the names under the sun. He had always called her names, routinely hit her, and yet she stayed with him because she said she had nowhere else to go.

Tommy went in the bookshop near the motorway, tried all the local charity shops, and of course there was never any sign of the book. One of the last things Terry said to Tommy was for him to keep looking, keep looking out for that hardback book with a little rip at the top of the spine, but Tommy knew he was pissing in the wind. Someone had had that envelope, and they were never letting on.

When Terry died, Tommy could see the relief in his

mum's face, like the relief they both felt when Terry went back inside, but deeper than that.

꙳

When Osborne died, after checking himself out of the hospital only to have a heart attack at home, the shop was closed and that was it. Osborne's kids had no interest in the business and Lee heard that they just recycled all the books, regardless of their worth, and sold the unit to the mechanics firm on the other side of the yard.

Lee had always known there was no redundancy coming. Like everyone else who'd ever worked there he'd never had a contract, and because when Osborne died they didn't get paid, he said he was dropped right in it, immediately having to figure out the Universal Credit system. Signing on had changed beyond all recognition since he'd last done it in the eighties, and he said he'd just about managed to survive until his first payment. For a while he said he'd done a lot of fishing, sometimes eating what he caught.

Warren had never needed the job anyway, was already flush from the money he'd been left, and so he just kept on cycling, getting more and more into it until he completed the Coast to Coast route which he said nearly killed him.

Virginia missed the shop. As with Lee, it had been a big part of her life, but she took the opportunity to make a change. She spent sixty grand on a chalet at Boat of Garten, went walking all year round in her beloved Scotland, going to spots she'd been with Norman, feeling his presence in all those quiet places. It was assumed she'd paid for it with the money Norman had left her.

Rubaiyat Man could often be found at the poetry night in The Farmer's Arms, where the landlady always enjoyed his performance. When one night he recited the whole of the *Rubaiyat of Omer Khayyam* it brought the house down, and the young kids who organized the night were amazed. The career of more than one young performance poet began that night. Rubaiyat Man was even able to afford to give up his electrician work to go freelance as a performance poet himself, and a highlight was when he supported John Cooper Clarke on a tour of West Yorkshire.

Ray's yellow van could still be seen going up and down the main road most days, and he'd always had other places to go to for a natter and a slash. That he could pay off the mortgage on his little terrace a couple of years ahead of schedule was something he wanted to shout from the rooftops about, but he'd finally learned to keep some things to himself.

Of course, there are no bookshops of these kinds around anymore, and as such, nowhere quite like them for people like these to go. Life is much more prescriptive, with computers dictating our choices and controlling our brains. But there once was a time when people bought books based on their own instincts and not algorithms, when they could wander around knackered old buildings with books in a kind of order but generally just scattered quixotically, by owners wilfully idiosyncratic in variously old fashioned human ways, in a time before we all walked headlong into this oblivion.

Licensed Premises

A s I walked in for the interview, I noticed a half empty glass of water on the table, left by the previous candidate. There were marks of her breath on the glass. Sitting down, I looked at the water again, but nobody on the panel moved. There were three academics: a woman, with a huge and justifiable chip on her shoulder about the marginalisation of women in literature, and two men. One of these men seemed to be impressed by everything I said. He was red faced and amiable. After my presentation, the woman, itching for intellectual debate, asked, what elevates this to master's level? Later, the other man on the panel asked, with something approaching a sneer, how do you situate yourself in the contemporary field?

Afterwards I walked down to Princess Street. Waiting at a pedestrian crossing I watched as the crowd of shoppers piled up on the other side, massing in the morning sunshine. My shirt was stained with sweat. I sat down on a bench in the shadow of the castle. Before the interview I'd googled the people on the panel. As far as I could tell, none of them had had any creative work published.

I dropped into Debenhams with the vague intention of

buying a new shirt. There were escalators and stairs among the white shining walls. Arrows pointed to 'Menswear', but after some fifteen minutes of walking I found myself in a cul-de-sac of suitcases. I started to walk more quickly and found myself back in a place I'd seen before, a corner of the store displaying shoes.

How do I get out? I said, to a middle-aged man standing by a tiny glass lift. I can't get out.

Oh, I know, it's terrible, I've known people stuck in here for days.

Eventually I walked out onto the blazing street. The walls of the castle glinted in the sun. I weaved my way through the tumult of people rushing for meal deals. I turned down a side street and walked along a quiet, cobbled road. There was a man standing outside a pub, smoking a thin cigar. Just go in, he said, smiling.

There was the bar, with six stools before it, and two sets of window seats with room for two people in each. Three of the stools were occupied, and a tall barman, the landlord, stood behind the counter, smiling. To the side of the bar there were wooden steps leading to a side room with tables. I had a look in there before deciding on a stool. I asked for a pint of Best and then perched myself at the end of the bar, near the window.

I sat quietly, listening to the sporadic conversation. When tourists came in, the bar came to life with a series of questions:

Is this the Rebus place?

Is Ian in?

Is he coming in later?

We want to try whisky. What do you recommend?

Is this a smooth whisky?

Do you have water, in it? Ice? How much?

Are single malts better?

One American couple stayed a while, but when the man pointed his huge camera at the landlord and the locals, they covered their faces and turned away in mock horror.

The landlord had sky blue eyes and a red nose. His shirt sleeves were rolled to the forearms and he pulled pints with big hands. He was a Celtic fan, and they'd lost a European tie to a bunch of part timers the night before.

Hey, Barry, at least in the next leg your boys will be able to get their gas boilers checked out, eh? said a little bloke called Alan, sitting in one of the other stools. No like the mighty Hibs!

I see Lennon's got banned already, I said.

Oh aye, said Alan.

I'm a Man City fan.

Oh, you're from Manchester? I went there once. Just the once, said Barry, with a wry smile.

I came for an interview at the university. Creative Writing, I said.

Oh, right?

So, I'm doing the literary pilgrimage.

You been to Milne's?

No, where's that?

Just on Hanover Street there.

That where MacCaig and them went?

Aye. But it's no like it was. There used to be loads of photographs and everything. I used to run it. It's changed now. But they've still got the Little Kremlin. Sorley MacLean, all of them used to sit in there and *orate*.

MacCaig was my primary school teacher, said the man who had been smoking the thin cigar outside. He was called Kenny.

Always had a glint in his eye when you saw him interviewed, I said.

Aye he did. That's because he was always pished, said Barry.

No, not always. But you're right, he liked a wee dram and a fag. And he did have a glint in his eye, said Kenny.

You know a pub called The Circus? said Barry.

Circus Tavern? I said.

That's right.

We're kind of twinned with that place. I went there once. Tiny place. Smaller than this.

Oh aye. But they still had a corner there they called a snug. It was incredible.

It's about the size of this room.

That's right.

I taught at Salford Uni. There's another good boozer there. The Crescent. Marx and Engels went in.

Dirty Old Town. Used to sing that when I knew Gerry. Who's that? I asked.

Gerry Rafferty, said Kenny.

Oh aye, said Alan.

Baker Street, I said.

He sang with Billy, said Kenny. The bumbleheads or something.

The Bumblebees, said Alan.

No, the Humble Bumbles, said Kenny.

The Hum Bumbles, oh, something like that. We sang on the same bill sometimes. Gerry was a nice fella.

I left my heart, by the gasworks wall, dreamed a dream, by the old canal . . . it was Barry again, singing the lyrics. Ewan McColl, I think.

Just then a couple of tourists came in. Do you do fish and chips here? they asked Barry.

Used to. But we stopped the food, he said.

Oh. But how does fish and chips work?

How does it *work*?

You put it on the plate? You could try Milne's if you like, they do food over there.

As they left, Barry bid them a fond farewell. How does if *fucking work?* he said, turning to the regulars.

So that's him up on the wall then? I said, as the laughter subsided.

Aye. But you see that John Hannah? He was shite in the role compared to the bloke Stott that came after. But you know Hannah bought shares in it all. He's no fucking stupid, said Alan.

Yeah, Ian bought the shares back, I think. Few years ago, said Barry.

I've never really watched it. Canongate's from here though, isn't it? I said.

That's right, aye. I knew the fella set that place up, said Kenny.

Aye, said Barry, you know Kenny here is our *cultural* role model. Look at them shoes, he said, leaning his head across the bar to grimace in the direction of Kenny's slip-ons. I have to say, they are a little *garish* for my tastes. Spring's a girl from the streets at night . . .

How's your gin and tonic? said Alan, to Kenny.

You want some more tonic? said Barry.

Oh, just give me a Guinness, for Christ's sake, said Kenny.

Good man, said Barry, to murmurs of approval all around.

Load of sugar in that tonic, anyway, said Alan.

So that's your diet gone, eh? said Barry.

I sipped from my pint and looked around. There was a TV high in the corner, covered in a thick film of dust, and a row of single malts below the optics. Above the optics there were two framed photographs, one of Ian Rankin and another of Ken Stott.

I smelled the spring on the smoky wind . . . my wife used to sing that part. Dirty old town, dirty old town . . .

So, do you know Mr Rankin then? I asked.

Ian, oh aye. Used to come in here when he didn't have a pot to piss in. I hope he comes in soon. I've got stacks of mail for him.

People just send it here?'

Aye. From all over. I'll chop you down, like an old dead tree . . .

Alan lumbered off a stool and made his way to the toilet.

Clouds are drifting, across the moon . . .

You see these tourists, they're good for business here. Good for Barry, so you can't complain too much, said Kenny. Oh, here's the brochure for the book festival.

Wonder if Ian's on it, said Barry.

I don't know, let me look. Oh aye, there he is.

You know I'll have to read something by him now I've come in here. What's the best one to start with? I asked.

Knots and Crosses, said Alan, returning from the toilet.

I looked at my watch and got another pint of Best. I

listened some more to the voices, the banter, the kind of company I'd missed. The afternoon had seemed to pass slowly compared to the morning. I imagined everyone rushing around outside. Sunlight shone on the optics, giving them a warm glow. Necking the last of my pint, I thought briefly of alternatives to the train.

I'll have to go, I said.

Oh, you're going? said Barry.

Yep.

Good luck with your job. Hope you get it, said Alan.

Aye, good luck, said Kenny, gulping his Guinness.

Aye, all the best, said Barry. Saw a train set the night on fire . . .

Cheers, I said, giving them the thumbs up as I walked back out onto the cobbled road.

People in suits commingled in the early evening sunshine. Hundreds waited to cross at the traffic lights near the train station, and on reaching the station rushed through the barriers to their respective platforms. I had a powerful urge to turn around, and so I did.

You're back then? said Barry.

Yep, missed it.

You missed the train? Can't you get the next one?

No, I got a cheap ticket. It was only valid for that one.

Get yourself a wee dram, said Kenny. I'm sure we'll think of something.

Might as well.

I sat back on the same stool as before and tried the Lagavulin. There was a lull in the conversation but the whisky warmed me. I could hear the gentle rubbing sound as Barry dried pint pots with a tea towel.

What elevates this pub to master's level? I asked. And how does this pub situate itself in the contemporary field?

Eh? said Barry.

If this pub . . . how does this pub elevate itself to master's level?

Okay . . . ? said Alan.

And how does this pub situate itself in the contemporary field?

When you say, situate itself in the contemporary field, asked Kenny, what do you mean?

Near the fucking window, said Alan.

No, no, no, Alan, come on, be fair. This is a *serious* question, said Barry. And this is what they asked you in the interview?

Yep.

And what did you say?

No, no, I'm asking you, what you'd say.

I'd say get another pint, said Alan.

No, no. I can go with this. I'd say that the pub speaks for itself, said Barry. And that my name is above the door. In letters above the door.

Fair enough, I said. So then, what elevates this place to master's level?

Master's?

Yeah.

Kenny here has a master's. But look at those *shoes*. Listen, this pub has a PhD, never mind a master's. But we don't need a PhD. Or a master's. If it was me, I would have told them that they were asking the wrong questions.

Sounds like bollocks to me, said Alan.

Alan, you're interrupting the *intellectual flow* here, said Barry.

Okay then, Barry, I said, what questions would *you* have asked?

Well, *now* you're asking. Let me just *cogitate* a moment here . . .

The Last Bookseller

WANDERING AROUND THE shop today I found this dead rat. Brown fucking bread and stiff as a board all spread-eagled in the fiction section. Shit me up a bit but then I just got the big sweeping brush and swept the cunt into the yard. Not the worse thing I've found. Human fucking faeces on the carpet. Someone in the shop had just crouched down and dumped in the TV bit.

What's worse than someone crapping on the carpet is these fuckers who come in and wander about in wide eyed wonder, saying it's an Aladdin's cave and all that bollocks, and then walk around the shop for an hour talking shite and then smile at you on the way out saying see you next time, after they've spent fuck all.

Funny fucking noises come from the roof sometimes. It's a tin roof sloping down but there's cats and squirrels and magpies and all sorts scurrying across it. Used to keep me awake but with ale down me I get a solid five hours every night, then wake up and for a split-second wonder where the fuck I am. Gets pitch fucking black in here but there's all these weird noises all the time and they don't bother me now. I think the roof expands and contracts and at first I was thinking fuck me there's ghosts.

It's pretty cosy in here tonight. I'm upstairs, right in the rafters, with my sleeping bag next to the oil heater. Fucking ace this sleeping bag, was give me by the son of this famous old British climber who'd died in the Himalayas and that. Duck down or whatever you call it. As long as you don't get it wet it's toasty as fuck.

The owner of this shop is fucking clueless. Was left to him by his old man and he's not arsed. He just sends random stuff out on What's App now and again. There was one time when people would leave us the occasional tip. Anyway, there was always a spare few quid knocking about in the till and we'd spend that on bog rolls and tea bags and washing up liquid and that. Old Richard never bothered but his lad's a tight bastard, is always on about us cutting costs.

I was coming back from the garage with a bagful of scran and I had to lock the gates behind me and this car pulls up, the lights blinding, and asks if we're open. I'm stood there locking the gate in the dark and I should have said, does it look like we're fucking open? Instead, I just said no, we're closed for the day but that we'll be open again at ten in the morning. He didn't even answer me then, didn't say thanks or anything, just drove off.

Bloke came in today. Started moaning about the fire exit being blocked and didn't I remember the fire from before? I said I didn't and told him not to worry about any fire. Said someone might report it. Anyone fucking does I'll know who it was won't I?

There's all these paintings hanging from the rafters in the shop, the old bloke Richard used to paint them and flog a few and then after a bit it seems nobody bought any anymore but they aren't bad, you know, realism, nothing abstract or anything. Sometimes after a couple of cans I'll stare at them pictures and wait for something to appear. I prefer abstract stuff in fairness. Last night the door of this remote Scottish bothy started to open and close but I reckon that was just to do with the ale.

Microwave meals and cans of lager every night take the edge off. The microwave meals aren't that bad these days either. I worked in this factory years ago and it was all curries, grim as fuck. Had a nice curry just now, tried all curries over the years but a Biryani is the one, you can't beat them. Not a microwave one, this one was from the takeaway, young lad on a bike from the Balti house calls to tell me he's here and I go out in the dark and take the padlock off the gate and get the ruby off him. First time he came he shit himself, but I mean they deliver everywhere these days with Deliveroo and Just Eat and that.

There's a little fridge in the kitchen for the milk and I have a bowl of Rice Krispies in the morning and then a bit of toast and some proper coffee. They've started selling it at the mill around the corner from here and it's a bit dear but well nice and I've got my little grinder for the beans. Today I didn't bother with lunch and just worked through and had a microwave cottage pie for tea.

Had to go in the brick hut today. The daddy long legs are crazy. There's a massive web stretching across the ceiling and over a couple of air vents. I had to get a book out from under them and I looked up at all these webs on the ceiling and I counted twelve of the fuckers, none of them moving, spooky as fuck. I got hold of the old brush in there and I poked at one of them with the brush handle and it started whirling around on the web trying to shit me up.

I'm lying in my sleeping bag sometimes and I swear to you I can hear books being moved around on the shelves. Middle of the night and it's like there's somebody there, fucking about in the sci-fi section. I think the beer makes me worse in some ways, get paranoid as fuck. Last night I got up out of the sleeping bag and I was wandering about in the dark and I turned the corner and nearly lost my shit when the corner of my eye caught the fucking mannequin.

I love it when the crows are on the roof. I close my eyes and I could be anywhere in the world, in Scotland maybe, some lonely fucking glen. Mrs never had any interest. She hated the dawn chorus and called them the twatty birds. But I love the fucking crows when they start calling across the rooftops.

There's this big mirror suspended from the rafters near the Philosophy bit and last night after a few beers I put all the shop lights on and lay under the mirror looking at myself. Was her leaving just an excuse to get shit-faced on a nightly basis, or was it because I was getting shit-faced on a nightly basis that she left? When you've got stuff like this on your mind you don't need Schopenhauer.

Fucking fire exit here is a joke, to be fair. Someone bought one of the coffee table hardbacks in front of it this morning. The extinguisher got used for some fucking fire years ago and never got replaced. It was put back in its rack on the wall after some scrotes lit rags and stuffed them through the letterbox.

Couldn't believe it today, had this cunt come round. He lives on the estate at the back and has a view of the shop and he says he knows I never leave. I say to him what does he want me to do about it? He says he knows the owner and he's going to tell him. I explain about my barney with the Mrs and how she fucked off and how I couldn't pay the rent on my own and the twat wasn't even listening. This is the kind of country we live in now. I asked this cunt what difference does it make if I'm living in the shop or not, what difference does it make to him, and he says well I'm using the electric and it will be costing Richard's lad money and I told him to keep his fucking nose out.

Another twat phoned up today and asked for a book from the travel bit so I went and had a look and though most of them look pretty new you look at the dates on them and it's like 2009 or whatever. Now that seems like yesterday to me but when you're going somewhere, especially a city, then you want a more up to date one and this fucker was wanting one for Rome and I knew before I even went and looked that we didn't have any recent ones for Rome because I had the last one a few years back. 2015 it was, Fodor's guide, mint condition. I had a look at some of the older ones, the Rough Guide one and the Lonely Planet one and I looked at some of the pictures of Rome like the Colosseum and St Peter's and all that and it took me right back there. Probably shouldn't have been thinking about my honeymoon, not healthy, but I realized I didn't have any pictures left.

Sold a few books on eBay again today. Decent little side-line that, manager doesn't even know about it, tops up my wages a treat. Got about five hundred in the bank now. Back in the black, most I've ever had. Going to keep saving.

Near the hotel in Rome there was this nice little Gelato

place. I was thinking about that today. We went end of September, still boiling but if you kept in the shade it wasn't too bad. And we got into this routine of having an air-conditioned siesta in the afternoon and then about five bells we wandered out and down the street to this Gelato place and the girl working there translated all the flavours for us. I had three lots of this ice cream with cream on top and the Mrs had the same and we sat on this little bench outside the Gelato place and by the time we finished, the ice cream would be melting on the pavement. We went back every day and tried all the different flavours and every time we walked past the shop the girl waved.

Pissing down here today. Last day in Rome there was this massive thunderstorm, and we stood there with the shutters open looking out of the hotel and the water fell on all these flowers and plants in the courtyard, the water just dripping from them and there was a breeze coming through the shutters and the sun was going in, was great just these black clouds pouring rain and it was all cool and nice.

Still raining here, been raining about a week now, constant noise on the tin roof. Massive puddles outside, depressing.

Went in the old brick hut again today. Brushed through a bit of web and it pissed me off. It had been pissing me off for a while walking through webs. Anyway today, I got the old sweeping brush and ran it along the ceiling in front of the webs and wiped out all the daddy long legs, swept them all away, swept all the webs away and killed every last one of the fuckers.

Lying in my sleeping bag last night I heard all sorts

going off, police cars with their sirens on speeding up and down the main road and then the helicopter kept coming over and for one minute I thought it was going to land in the yard, it felt that close. When I got up this morning, I wasn't sure if it had been a dream or real and when I looked up the local paper on Twitter to see if they'd done anything about it there was no report of anything happening round here. Funny how you think everything bad that happens is going to be on the news.

Day one of knocking the ale on the head. No more booze for me from now on. But we'll take it one day at a time. I'm not an alkie or anything, I never have been, but I just want to see if anything changes from it.

After it pissed down in Rome, the Mrs got bit to fuck by the mosquitoes. That's all she ever said about our honeymoon.

There's a painting at the top of the stairs which I didn't see for years and then I started noticing it. One night when I was still on the ale I dreamed about it. It's not one of Richard's, it's a reproduction of a Munch I think it is and it's this topless woman with dark hair and it's a beautiful painting, especially when you look in the dark. She was beside me in the dream and I didn't want to wake from it, it was so warm, and I woke up and that warmth was spreading all over me.

Great day in the shop today. Bloke in the states wants me to send him scans of this book. We always put clear descriptions of the books on the websites but cunts like this want pictures. I wouldn't mind but we were only selling the book for four quid. So, I scanned a picture of the front cover, the back cover, the contents page and the index. Need to do this shit all the time and the cunts don't get back to you.

Was looking for some other pictures I'd scanned when I found a load of images on the computer of the shop like it used to be. Fucking line of people at the counter in the days before the internet.

All day long today I waited for the phone to ring, sat looking at the order screens, clicked from one to the other, refreshed them over and over. In the end there was fuck all to do so I finally lit the rags.

Magpie Court

ONE NIGHT OVER whisky they decided they'd have a go at putting together their own small press magazine, Simon taking care of the writing, Niamh the art.

Simon had had loads of stuff published in these kinds of magazines and they all had daft names like *Rain Cat*, *Obsessed with Copper*, *Buck Teeth*, *Strumpet Tree*, *Iambic*, *Prisoner 32*, *Skint Press*, *Smokefires* and *Dream Weaver* and were run by one or two people, usually writers themselves, who set up these magazines and appointed themselves editors. All you needed was a printer, a load of paper and a big stapler and you had a magazine ready to be filled with work.

For years, Simon had sent his work out to magazines like these. Sometimes you got a quick reply that said no, sometimes you didn't get a reply for months. Sometimes you never heard back, sometimes there was the pointless rigmarole of edits back and forth through the post that were just Simon fighting the editor into a stalemate. Occasionally there was that magical moment, where, printed on a little strip of paper or handwritten across the bottom of work sent back, the editor said they very much liked his story or poem and would be delighted to publish it in the forth-coming issue.

For the name of their new magazine, he suggested Magpie Court, the name of the flats he lived in, and Niamh said that would do for now, until they thought of something better. They printed up some flyers and dropped them off in places all over town: pubs, bars, record shops, market stalls, tattoo parlours. A little piece of paper, a quarter the size of a sheet of A4, it had a sketch of the tower block drawn by Niamh, and Simon's address as the place to send work.

Submissions would be slow until people began to hear about the magazine so they decided to put some of their own work in the first issue, stipulating in the editorial that they would only be doing it this one time. Simon hated those magazines that were an ego trip for the self-appointed editors, pious bastards who acted like they knew it all because they'd read one volume of Proust or written a sestina. In one magazine that he sent to, the editor incorporated Simon's story into one big story of his own so that Simon's work was no longer attributed to him. The guy must have had some balls. That magazine disappeared after three issues, but the guy had had Arts Council funding right from the off. It was unbelievable really, but in those days they handed out money left, right and centre.

Next job was trying to get the magazine into some shops. Some places just said no immediately. There was this big shop that sold expensive art magazines that were all about the design and when they looked at the low production values of *Magpie Court*, a stapled a5 booklet with a black and white reproduction of one of Niamh's paintings on the front, it didn't matter to them how great the writing was inside.

There was this other shop on the corner of the street near the train station and the guy behind the counter had worked there for years, little bald fella with an earring and a cheeky goatee who let Simon stand there for ages reading the lit mags.

You alright, chief?

Yeah, what can I do for you?

I've got this new magazine that we're doing.

Cool.

Have a look at them, said Simon, passing five copies over the counter.

They look decent these.

Cheers. Will you stock them then?

Have you got an invoice?

Erm, no.

Well, I'll keep hold of these and if you bring an invoice in then we can put it all through the accounts and that.

Okay and how much do you take?

Forty percent.

Jesus.

Just the way it is, cocker.

Okay, no worries, I thought maybe thirty, thirty-five?

Always been forty in here.

No worries.

I see you've got some decent writers.

Yeah.

I like the cover as well, very striking.

Yeah, that's Niamh, she does the art stuff.

Oh right, so it's art as well?

Yeah.

Cool.

Cheers.

So, you're Simon?

Yeah.

I'm Henry.

Nice one, Henry, Simon said, shaking his hand. So, are you a writer?

Yeah, I dabble here and there. TV mostly.

Oh right.

Have you been published then?

Oh yeah, he said. It was the first question anyone asked when he told them he was a writer.

I've had a few bits and pieces on TV. One-offs mainly but I'm working on this sitcom.

Right.

It's hard though, I'm here five days a week and it takes me an hour here and back on the train and by the time I've done all that I'm too knackered for writing.

I know what you mean. Anyway, I better be off.

Cheers, cocker.

Cheers, Henry.

꧁꧂

Monday morning he'd stare at the hills, even if it was pissing down, wishing he was a farmer or something, just wandering the fells and pleasuring cows or whatever it was they did. Imagine the joy of not having to say good morning to a load of people you didn't even care about in an office you didn't want to be in, completing routine, repetitive tasks with the only solace being that it was easy and paid the rent and meant you didn't have to deal with the dole office.

There was a massive clock on the fifth floor, huge digital numbers in red that glowed across the carpet on all the dark days. Simon couldn't stop looking at it. There was that clock, then the clock on his phone, the time in the bottom right-hand corner of the work computer, and the time on his watch. Counting down the minutes to break time, or lunch time, or afternoon break. And the days were the same, the grim inevitability of Monday morning, trying not to think about what day it was until at least Wednesday lunchtime, the halfway point of the week, and then the gradual brightening towards weekend, when the sad sacks around him started to crack a smile.

He got up when he liked on Saturday and did whatever he wanted all weekend, with work almost totally out of his mind until Sunday night after his tea, when the dread started creeping up again. Millions of people had got used to it, that was just the way it was. But anyone who did it on a permanent basis had given up on their dreams, transferred those dreams into the consolations of kids and mortgage, providing security for their babies, consoling themselves that their dreams had been selfish and that they had transcended those dreams to become selfless, better people.

One Saturday morning, Simon was in for a bit of overtime, unusual for him. There were only a few others in, and the bus had been great, much less people on it coughing and spluttering their guts up, and town was quieter too, he had a chance to look up at the nice old brick buildings before they got bulldozed for progress.

He had the lift to himself on the way up to the fifth

floor and there was no-one on reception and he was left to his own devices. After morning break, he went down the corridor to the photocopier room, took the magazine out of his rucksack and then printed out fifty copies. At lunchtime he finished work and walked out of there with a much heavier rucksack. On his way to the bus stop he went into a stationary shop and bought a long arm stapler.

When he got home, he started putting the magazine together, laying out the pages in order across the floor before folding the A4 sheets in half and stapling them into an A5 booklet. Even after just fifty copies, his arms were aching from the sorting, and he had a blister in the palm of his hand from the stapling.

They'd had some decent submissions, funny how word got round. There were some short stories from the pint-sized maestro Donald Gibson, poetry by American underground figure Sale Waterside and lots of stuff by writers never published before, and this was the great thing, the whole point of the magazine. It was an outlet for new writers, somewhere to send your work, and Simon kept his ego out of it.

Niamh had provided a great cover, a reproduction of a triptych she'd done called *Three Fuckwits in a Boat*, featuring prominent politicians getting twatted with paddles.

There was a guy worked at the Uni and they met up one night in The Shakespeare. This bloke was called Nigel and taught in the humanities and had had a book of articles published. This book was a hundred pages long, cost eighty odd quid and sold four copies in seven years. Nigel carried it around in his man bag at all times of the day and night and if anyone asked him what he did for a living he just tossed the book at them. Simon tried reading it but couldn't follow the Latin.

Nigel got the beers in because Nigel always got the beers in and Simon got shit-faced for free.

So how is your journal selling?

No idea, Nigel. It's not about that.

I've seen it in Henry's, and in one or two places around town.

Yeah. It's doing okay.

Are you going to apply for funding?

I'm not arsed about that. But yeah, we're getting an intern from your place, student wants experience in publishing.

Good idea.

Yeah. We need more submissions though really.

Takes time.

I guess so. I don't want to be one of those editors fills it up with my own work. I hate that shit.

I might have something.

Oh right.

A short story. I've been working on it for ten years.

What's it about?

Well, it's hard to distil in a sentence.

Nigel sent the story about a week later. It started well and was beautifully written, but it went on for page after page. Simon could only staple together about sixty pages and explained that he couldn't have one story taking up forty of them.

A bit later some students at the Uni started their own magazine and they had Nigel's story in there. It was a nice-looking magazine: glossy cover, good quality printing inside, high production costs, well-crafted writing honed to dullness.

When Niamh the perfectionist finally got the next issue ready, after a six month wait during which Simon felt they lost a fair bit of momentum in terms of sales and interest, she said she wanted to organize a proper launch night. Funny, she wouldn't pay for a launch of any of the issues he'd edited but now it was her turn things were different.

They booked a room in The Shakespeare. Somehow Niamh had wangled it for free. They'd been flyering for a good couple of weeks, all over town.

At eight there was nobody there, and the landlord, hoping for more beer sales in exchange for letting out one of his rooms for free, was starting to look a bit anxious. Add to it that all the poets reading got a paper wristband entitling them to one free drink and he wasn't looking at a profitable night.

At about half eight the first of the poets showed up on his bike. He walked in with his high viz jacket on, pulling folded up bits of paper from his rucksack. He was okay and Simon might have expected him to turn up first. At about nine the rest of them floated in, ironically oblivious to anything going on around them. Most of them were poets who wrote about themselves and they stood around at the bar all waiting to be bought a drink, and when nothing happened they started fishing in their pockets or bags for coins. It was sad how happy they all looked when Simon turned up with the wristbands. These people needed to get jobs. Instead they sponged off the dole and swanned around in café's while Simon had to endure the fifth floor. The exception was Frank Campbell and his Wurlitzer. Frank worked for the council and paid his way but couldn't make it this time.

The landlord looked almost suicidal as he poured one frothing pint after another of Krombacher and his mood didn't improve when he watched the poets all nursing those pints for most of the night.

Henry Miller said it made people feel better about themselves to buy drinks for others, so you could justify it that way, and when Dermot Bridge turned up, a man who apparently worked for the government in some scientific capacity and was loaded, the poets perked up no end. He got the beers in, even a few whiskies at the end of the night, and everyone was happy.

All night the poets had been hassling Simon about publishing their stuff in the next issue. It was funny, none of them ever talked to him before he set up the magazine, now he couldn't get them to go away. And there were always new people turning up. This lad who looked like Alan Bennett and talked like Nigella Lawson had produced his own chapbook and had twenty copies of them in his bag. He kept asking Simon to look at a copy, but Simon said it was best to just send his poems in to the magazine. When Simon went to the bogs and locked himself in, this lad followed him and started waving his poems under the toilet door.

When everybody eventually went home, at about two in the morning, Simon helped the landlord stack the chairs on the tables and then assessed the night. Apart from the poets nobody had turned up, but they had had a good time among themselves and applauded each other in an atmosphere of apparent camaraderie. They all seemed to copy a certain way of reading – adopting the dreaded 'poet voice' – and there was the usual competitiveness, people who were supposed to get ten minutes waffling on for half an hour until you had to drag the selfish cunts off. But the real trouble with poets was they had no money and there was no real audience for poetry. All the poets had taken their free copies and nobody else had paid for a single copy. When he talked to Niamh about it the next day, she started banging on about the Arts Council again.

The magazine was doing okay in terms of online sales and Simon would take a big batch of post to the post office in the centre of town and send a load out. They cost about fifty odd pence a time to post. It was only the odd one that went abroad that cost more.

They had stuff sent from all over the USA, Canada, and most memorably, the island of Aruba, by some guy called Gregory Brooms, a cracking prose poem. They all got a free contributor copy and these were the more expensive to post out. But it was great, sitting high up in a council flat and getting post through his door from all over the world.

Simon got the third issue together pretty quickly. There were some regular contributors. It wasn't so much that he wanted to publish the same people in every issue, it was just that these guys kept sending in the best work. Of course, Simon had his favourites, he was only human, and pretty much any writer from America usually got in. There was this bloke called Bear Bingham from South Bend, Indiana and it was this great stuff about working in factories, a mixture of Fred Voss and Philip Levine.

Simon went to the shop near the train station and checked on how many copies had been sold and two out of the five had gone. Henry wasn't in and there was a young woman behind the counter. It was always so quiet in there, bit weird, even a bit awkward as he stood there looking through some more magazines where the editors published their own work.

He picked up *Magpie Court* and realized that what he'd done was work in opposition to these other magazines. There were low production values and most of the writers were newly published, and there were working class voices, black voices, voices from all over the world.

❧

One day he saw Frank Campbell on the street, briefcase in hand and looking as depressed as everyone else on a Tuesday.

You okay, Frank? said Simon.

Alright, lad?

You had a good day at work?

Actually no, I haven't.

Sorry about that. I've heard the council are decent to work for.

Whoever told you that mustn't have worked for the council.

Thought they looked after you?

That's nonsense. They look after themselves, the bosses, big rises every year and our wages stay the same, or well, they get worse with the inflation of course.

Stick with the Ginsberg, mate.

I will do, he said, perking up. You know I've got a studio set up in my bedroom now, sound proofed and everything. I can work all night.

You ever been married, Frank?

Oh yeah, years ago, but I'm done with all that. I'd rather read Ginsberg now. Garcia Lorca, what are you doing with those watermelons, you dirty Spanish bastard.

Eh?

You never read *A Supermarket in California*?

Oh yeah, that's one of the best ones.

Indeed it is, young man.

Didn't you read that one last time?

I take sections of it, intersperse it with my Wurlitzer tone poems.

Splendid.

When's your next launch?

Be a month or so.

Oh great. I'll send you some stuff.

Okay great.

In fact, I've got some in my suitcase.

Better if you just send them in to the magazine.

But then I'll have to pay for a stamp. It's easier this way, just let me find some.

He opened the suitcase and there were dozens of sheets

of paper in there, scrawled with doodles and drawings, and Frank messed around for ages before sorting some out.

They're the best ones.

Alright, Frank.

Thanks, lad.

⚜

Simon was working on the next issue when he got an email from Nigel asking to meet up. He said he wanted to discuss something very important, and possibly very damaging, but he didn't want to do it by email.

Nigel was into his second pint before he finally got to the point.

There's a poet in your magazine. Frank Campbell?

Oh yeah?

How well do you know him?

We have a few pints now and again. Nice guy.

I see, okay. Well, the thing is, and this is a delicate point, so I just want to make sure that we are fine to discuss it.

Of course.

You're absolutely sure?

Yes.

I don't want us to fall out over this.

I wish you'd get to the point, Nigel.

Well, it's . . . I don't want you to take it the wrong way. Okay well, look, it has come to my attention that Campbell, in a word, is something of a plagiarist.

In what way?

Well, one of the poems in your last issue, and another from issue two, I think.

Really?

Yes, it seems that way.

How do you know?

Well, I've had this email.

What email?

Chap calls himself 'the poetry detective'.

Are you having a laugh?

No.

Who is this guy?

I don't know. But he's all over the papers. He contacted me because we've known each other for years. He knows I'm based here, thought I might know about the magazine.

So you know his name then?

Yes.

What's he called?

Jeremy.

Jeremy?

Look, he emailed me a breakdown of both poems. I printed them out. He doesn't have any axe to grind with you, you can be sure of that. Here's the two poems you've printed, and here's the originals, he said, passing the papers to Simon.

Simon read through them. It seemed undeniable. Cheeky bastard, he said.

And these aren't the only ones. Jeremy has looked at all of Campbell's poems he can find.

It must just be a mistake. Like he didn't remember where the lines were from, or something.

Well, I think you're being favourable there, Simon.

I'm going to speak to him about it first, the cheeky bastard. I mean, this damages the magazine as well.

Certainly could.

Christ's sake.

Time for another drink I would say. Care for another?

Dead right.

So, you say there's more? said Simon, when Nigel came back from the bar.

Apparently. Mainly in Australia I think, Australian poets he's ripped off, I mean.

Jesus.

⁂

A few days later, Simon met up with Frank again.

Alright, lad?

No, I'm not alright, Frank.

What's the score?

I'll tell you what the score is, fuckface, you've been ripping off other people's poems.

Hey, first of all, you don't talk to your elders like that, Simon. And second, where's your proof?

I'll show you the proof, grandad, it's here.

Frank looked through the papers, at first looking puzzled, then a little angry, then shaking his head.

Seems like you have me bang to rights.

Doesn't it?

I'd say so.

What's the point, Frank?

I don't know.

I mean, none of us is making any money, I can't ever imagine doing that, I mean, what's the point? Even if nobody else knows, *you* know it isn't yours.

What can I say, Simon?

How can you explain it? It's just cheating, isn't it?

Well, I can explain it and I can't.

I'm waiting.

It's influence, isn't it? I've read a lot of poems over the years and so the influence just seeps through. Look close enough and you'll probably find lines from Ginsberg and Lorca in there too. There's nothing new anymore.

Oh, come on Frank, the poems that I put in *Magpie Court* are just rip offs.

I don't know, must just have been the influence.

Cheating.

Intertextuality.

What?

The academics call it intertextuality. If I'm being honest, I sometimes use poems for their structure, and I might take some phrases here and there. I've been doing it for years, lad. Call it a reworking, poetic versioning, whatever you like.

I feel a right mug.

It's influence, not plagiarism. Folk singers have done it for centuries. You borrow bits here and there. And it's only poetry for Christ's sake, there's only about twenty people read it in the country anyway.

This Jeremy's coming after you, Frank. They call him the poetry detective.

Poetry detective? Ridiculous.

Seems like he's on a bit of a crusade.

It will pass over, lad, don't worry.

❧

When the article came out, the poetry world, small as it is, was in uproar. A pious bunch at the best of times, the poets, and the university poets in particular, took this as an opportunity to stick the boot in while establishing their own holier than thou credentials. It didn't seem to matter to anyone that *Magpie Court* only sold about thirty copies an issue, there was no perspective. It was outright condemnation.

It emerged that Frank had once received a grant from the Arts Council on the back of his published output, at least half of which now seemed dubious in origin. He'd also done a Master's degree in Creative Writing, and his thesis had been available in the library, but now the university had removed it. There were howls of anger about the Arts Council grant, which people said he would have to pay back. He had been booked to read at a number of places, including a couple of festivals, and these invitations were all withdrawn to a murmured chorus of approval.

❧

It was funny, when Simon looked through some of his own published poems, he saw among them a clear rip off of some Bob Dylan lyrics, and he really couldn't be sure if this had been done deliberately. The more he thought about it the more he had to admit he had just nicked those two lines from a Dylan song. It seemed only a matter of time before Jeremy was on to him too.

It seemed that this Jeremy spent all his time searching for examples of plagiarism in poetry, and there were more newspaper articles. Increasingly, the articles began to be about Jeremy, rather than the plagiarism issue. He was interviewed at home, spoke about the collapse of his marriage. It seemed maybe that this plagiarism thing had given him something to focus on outside that collapse. Perhaps he'd done something wrong within the marriage and now he was trying to rectify the karma. He was relentless, and poet after poet was exposed, and the writers of the original poems were almost always absolutely outraged. One said he felt violated.

※

Simon met up with Frank again. Frank was at a low ebb and Simon thought a couple of pints would help the mood.

How are things, Frank?

Bad times, Simon.

I'm sure it will all wash over soon.

It won't, believe me.

They do seem to be focusing on you more than anyone else.

I wonder why?

What do you mean?

I don't want to play the race card.

I'm not following.

Whitey is outraged.

Eh?

I'm the only black poet involved in this scandal, but the focus is on me, is still on me. They aren't saying anyone else needs to pay their grant back.

That's not going to happen, Frank.

You know I've had death threats, hate mail. I don't know

how they know my address but I've had poison pen letters. They put my picture in the papers and they always refer to me as 'black poet' Frank Campbell, what's that about?

Who are these death threats from?

Obviously they never put their names.

This is all getting ridiculous, Frank.

It is what it is.

Well, I will still publish you, just don't embarrass me.

I'm grateful to you, Simon.

Everyone makes mistakes, everyone deserves a second chance. This isn't fucking Salem.

Thank you, Simon. I just hope the council see it that way.

You'll be fine.

Let's hope so.

⚜

Simon had put together some short stories influenced by Shirley Jackson's *The Lottery*, and a guy he'd published in the first couple of issues of *Magpie Court* emailed and said that a publisher he knew was looking for short story collections, and if Simon emailed him the stories, he would forward them on. It was a curious thing, Simon had not started the magazine to curry favour, but found that by publishing people's work he made allies. The downside was that every time he had a pint with one of these people it would always get back to the magazine and the poems or stories they had sent to Simon. He wondered if they would still be around when the magazine ended.

As for the people whose work he rejected for the magazine, well, their hatred was palpable. He'd see them out and about and they'd just ignore him. Sometimes *Magpie Court* would get slagged off in other magazines.

It was interesting though, seeing the submissions process from the other side. Some people would send poems and Simon just didn't like their style and never would, and these people kept on sending more and more, week after week, in the hope of wearing him down. But the more they sent the less likely he was to publish them. Eventually he told this one guy to come back in a year and received a vitriolic response along the lines of *Magpie Court* being a crap magazine in which Simon only published his friends and that Simon himself was a joke of a human being who was going to get cancer.

❧

Simon and Frank met up again for a pint.

Hi Frank, how's it going?

We keep on keeping on.

Yeah, what can I get you?

I'll have a Guinness.

Guinness? Okay I'll join you.

When Simon got back with the drinks, Frank was still taking off more layers. He must have had about four coats on and yet never wore a hat.

I'm still not getting any readings, he said.

I was going to ask you about that.

That poetry detective has killed me.

I'm sad to hear that, pal.

It's racism.

How is it racism? I publish you, don't I?

You can't understand.

Why can't I?

Because you're white.

I have loads of black friends.

Of course you do.

Half of my writing heroes are black.

I'm not talking about you, I'm not talking personally about you, it's not about you. It's whiteness.

What?

Whiteness. Ask them at the uni about it. You can't understand how I feel because you are white. You are privileged.

Privileged? How the hell am I privileged?

Not you personally.

I haven't got a pot to piss in. How can I be privileged?

I'm not going to explain it to you.

Why not, I'd like to know how the hell I'm privileged.

Google it. I'm not explaining it to you.

How do you expect me to learn?

You learn for yourself.

Why don't you tell me?

I've spent my whole life trying to explain it. Now I put it in my poems.

Yeah right.

What's that supposed to mean?

When you put it in a poem you've ripped off from someone else, you mean.

That's out of order, Simon.

You're out of order.

Fuck you, Simon, said Frank, before putting his coats back on.

Don't be daft, Frank.

I'm going, he said, finishing off the Guinness.

Wear a hat, Frank.

What?

Wear a hat.

Oh fuck off, Simon.

For the next issue of *Magpie Court*, Simon was planning to include three poems by Frank, and he was also working on an editorial in defence of Frank and condemning the witch hunts that were going on. Simon had googled 'whiteness' and started to get his head around what Frank had said about privilege.

There was some good stuff coming in the new issue. There was a series of flash fictions by this American writer from Florida and Simon hadn't even heard of flash fiction. It seemed they were stories of less than a thousand words. The likes of Kafka and Hemingway had written them years ago but 'flash' was a new term for them, a marketing gimmick that seemed to be working. There was some Oulipo cobblers, a bunch of confessional poems set in the city from a locally famous woman who had once been homeless, a short story sent in from a bloke in Canada, some long poems by a poet from South Africa, and one or two apprentice pieces by local writers Simon wanted to give first publication to. That was the biggest buzz, publishing people for the first time. He couldn't make head or tail of the Oulipo stuff, but he was adamant about not just publishing stuff he liked. If it seemed good, then he was happy to publish it. And if he didn't want to publish it, he found that 'not quite right for the magazine' was the kindest way to phrase rejection.

❧

When Frank turned up in the pub, Simon got him a Guinness. Then he fished into his rucksack and showed Frank the rough copy of the next issue, asked Frank to read through his poems and check for typos.

How have you been, Frank?

I'm totally skint, and lost my job at the council, but apart from that, fine.

Oh shit, I never realized.

Whole bunch of redundancies.

Sorry to hear it, Frank.

They've been threatening it for years. Working for the council is not what it was.

Shit.

And it happened at the worst time.

How do you mean?

Well I've lost all my gigs haven't I?

Of course, yeah. I'm sorry, Frank.

I don't blame you, Simon, you're okay. It's these other pious bastards. Never made a mistake in their lives. Sod them. Glass houses and all that.

What do you mean, Frank?

I mean if I ever meet that poetry detective, I'm going to tell him to get a life.

He was on something the other day, going on about it again.

You know what that is Simon? You know what it is, and I hadn't heard this phrase before, but it's what they call 'virtue signalling.'

How do you mean?

Well it's like he's saying, look at me, I'm doing all this research off my own back just to find out if someone somewhere has used a bit of someone's else's poem. What a great guy I am.

Oh right.

People like that have got dark secrets, man.

I'd not thought of it like that. I thought maybe he just wants to be liked.

Nobody does nothing for nothing in this world. That poetry detective is either trying to make up for something or trying to get something out of it in the future.

I know but you did copy someone else's poem, Frank.

It's like I killed someone!

Nobody's saying that.

That's how it feels, Simon. And I might as well have killed someone, to be honest. I've lost all my gigs and my regular job. Can't get a gig for toffee.

I know but losing your council job has nothing to do with the plagiarism thing though.

How do you know, Simon? How do you know that the poetry detective hasn't been on to the council? Or that someone at the council saw something online? They've always hated that I'm a poet, Simon, on top of being black. I should never have told anyone at the council because they throw it back in your face any chance you get. I'm telling you, wherever you work, never tell them you're a writer.

I don't.

Very wise.

So what you going to do for work?

I'm signing on, aren't I?

Right.

I've done it before and I'll do it again, they've had plenty of tax out of me over the years. Never thought I'd be back here.

Sorry, Frank.

I still reckon I've give them more tax than they've give me.

Probably. Anyway you having another Guinness, Frank?

Yes please, lad. Might as well.

Jeremy won a big poetry award for his new collection *Sounds, Familiar*. He got a large cash prize and lots of media coverage, and when Simon saw this Jeremy on breakfast TV he couldn't help thinking of Frank.

It hadn't made the national news that Frank was last seen walking towards the river, but they did bring up the poetry detective stuff.

So tell us about the title then, Jeremy, one of the present-ers said, holding the book up to the camera. It's hard not to connect that with your sleuthing work as the poetry detective. Actually, we should just explain to our viewers, for those who don't know, that Jeremy, it's fair to say, got a bit of a name of himself, became known as the poetry detective. Do you want to say a bit more about that?

Well, basically I was exposing people as plagiarists.

Can you say a little more?

Yes, I can. It is a sad reality in the poetry world that sometimes people cheat, and it came to my attention that the work of a poet I once appeared alongside in a magazine and actually once vouched for in a competition, so that he won a not insubstantial amount of money, he had actually plagiarized a lot of his work from poets in other countries, in this particular case, Australia.

I find this fascinating, I have to say.

Well, in a way it is, but in others it is defaming the name of poetry, undermining the integrity of poetry.

But I suppose it's like, well, some people might say, who's going to know?

Well precisely, it's just that I discovered I had a particular gift for it, not sure why. Just the way my brain works. I can remember words, phrases, patterns of words and phrases, patterns of lines. It comes quite easy for me and so it is not difficult for me to see this kind of thing when it occurs.

I see.

I mean at the end of the day they know it is not their own work.

Why do it then?

Well, there's money to be made isn't there? Places to be published, prizes to win, jobs in academia to go for.

I hadn't thought about that.

People don't, that's half the problem. And then there's the people who are doing this fairly, and maybe they miss out on that prize or that job in academia.

Well, you've won this prize haven't you? I'm just wondering if you think your work as the poetry detective ultimately helped you win this prize?

I don't understand.

Can't have done you any harm?

There's no connection between the two things as far as I'm aware.

But I mean, the title seems to suggest a connection.

That's purely coincidental, I mean, if you read the titular poem of the collection, you'll see that it's an entirely euphonic celebration.

The Meadows

T HE MAN IN the blue Transit sat behind the wheel looking out across the fields. He'd been coming every day for a week. The girl hadn't been back since he saw her walking the dog the Monday before. It was the summer holidays and there were kids everywhere. He kept on drinking his coffee, having finished his sandwich. There was sweat on his brow and, as he looked out across the fields, he saw the girl skipping along, then throwing a stick for a brown dog with floppy ears. He had a Jack Russell that tear-arsed around the cabin of the Transit, kept him company when he was driving for work. He let out Teresa, and she immediately ran over to the dog with floppy ears, baiting it. The girl tried to get her dog on the lead and Transit van man came to the rescue, helped by getting Teresa on the lead. The girl said thanks, and he said that her dog looked thirsty. He had some water, thought her dog should have some. She hesitated slightly, then followed him up the hill to where the van was parked, watched as he opened the side door of the Transit. He started filling the dog bowl with water. When it was filled, he watched as the girl walked slowly forward with her dog still on the lead, and as the dog sipped slowly at the water he pushed her into the van, dog and all, and slid the door shut, locked it. The girl started screaming so he went round to the back of the van, climbed in that way, walked towards the girl, cornered her, made her stop. The dog was still growling so he kicked it in the ribs. It fell out of the back of the van. He taped up the girl's mouth, tied her up, left her lying there on a mattress as he got out of the back, locked the door then climbed back in the cabin to drive off. He took a last look around the fields and there was nobody there except two lads playing football.

At the petrol station she listened as he put the petrol in and then when she heard him walking away she tried the side door of the blue Transit, backing up to the latch and pressing down on it with her bound hands. By some miracle it was open, and she used her foot to slide it across. The open side door was on the other side of the blue Transit, so she couldn't be seen from the petrol station. She ran across the forecourt, crossed the main road, hid behind a bush in a field of wheat. She watched through the bush as the man came out. He was big, fat and bald, and he came waddling out of the petrol station and got in the blue Transit, before getting out again and closing the side door. He stood there looking around, then seemed to think better of it and got back in the blue Transit before driving off at speed down the A road.

The man got out of the blue Transit van and shut the garage door from inside, then went round to the side of the van and slid open the door and she wasn't there. She wasn't fucking there. He stood there looking at the empty space in the van. How hadn't he noticed? This was a nightmare.

He told himself to stay calm, thought back, how did she get out with the central locking? Had he left the door open? Why the fuck did he go for petrol with her in the back? It was like he'd been in a kind of daze, in denial of what he was doing, just acting normal like getting petrol. But where had she gone, why didn't he notice she was not in the back? Why didn't he check? He had been stupid, a fucking amateur.

He needed a different kind of van, one where he could see into the back from the driver's seat, and more importantly he needed to fucking get rid of this van anyway, because the girl would remember the colour of it. He'd get a white van, get on Auto Trader or whatever, flog the blue van, get a white van, then he'd be a white van man among thousands of white van men. He was staring at the empty space in the back of the van, then he went for the hose, turned the brass tap on at the wall, rinsed down the back of the van, turned off the tap, listened to all the water dripping, clicked off the garage light, went back in the house, got a can of lager from the fridge.

There was one time before he could sell it when he got pulled over in the van for speeding, and the police did check in the back. But nothing came of it.

All he'd had to do was take his time, be patient, and then one day there she was, another little girl walking down the back path near the railway line. He walked from the van, grabbed her, held her mouth, dragged her across the meadows. Broad daylight, nobody around, took less than five minutes and this time he tied her hands and legs up, taped her mouth, locked the back of the van, didn't go for petrol, drove home, put the van straight in the garage, closed the garage door.

His plan was to take her into the house, upstairs, into the bedroom, but in the back of the van he lost his temper, she wouldn't shut up until he hit her in the face, and as she was lying there crying he did what he wanted.

Leaving the loud music on in the kitchen, he went down to the cellar, closed the door behind him and walked down the stone steps. He clicked on the light and then lifted the little white body down off the peg, lowering the crumpled limbs onto the cold stone floor.

Afterwards, he left her lying there while he unfurled various plastic sheets and lined them up together, and then he got the saw started and began cutting up her body into more manageable pieces. Once he'd done that, he started taping up the various plastic sheets with body parts in them, and when he'd taped up all the parts in plastic sheets he rested the packages against the wall in a neat line. Going to the opposite wall he turned on the little bronze wall tap, lifted the green hose and started spraying down the floor. Walking back over to the tap he turned it off, stood there listening to the dripping water and the muffled sound of loud music. He glanced up at the bare peg and walked back up the stone steps, clicked off the light and closed the cellar door behind him, before walking into the kitchen to turn off the stereo.

He got all the ingredients out of the cupboard, the ras el hanout, cumin, harissa, ground ginger, tin of chickpeas, chopped lamb, then got an onion and a few cloves of garlic, began chopping the onion while the olive oil warmed in the casserole dish. When all the ingredients were in the pot, he brought them to a simmer then turned the heat down and put the lid on the pot, and even with the lid on the pot soon the whole house was filled with the smell of the chorba. He left it as long as he could, almost an hour before spooning a big portion out into a bowl.

He came off the A road, took the roundabout past the Asda and then followed the road through the deserted centre of the village to the turn off up the hill. He climbed the steep gradient with his lights on full beam as there were no street lights now. He reached the brow of the hill, saw the bright city lights in the distance, and then went down the hill in the darkness and parked the van. He slid open the side door and picked up one of the packages of black plastic and tape, rested it against the side of the van, took out the spade then slid the door shut. He could see his own breath in the moonlight and was glad of the gloves. He struggled to lift the package then had it on his shoulder, grabbed the spade in his other hand and then walked the footpath in the moonlight before veering off under the trees, beneath where all the crows were nesting. He looked again at the pattern of trees, could see beyond them the lights of a farmhouse. He started digging, and when the hole was deep enough placed the package into it.

Carrying the spade, he met up with the moonlit foot-path. Back in the van he started the engine, cranked up the heating, looked up and down the road, made his way back over the brow of the hill, but didn't go back past the supermarket, instead taking the long way round, avoiding the centre of the village, where he knew there was CCTV, and driving in a long sweeping C around the hills before meeting up again with the A road which took him out of the countryside and back to the suburbs.

Reeks

I

O N HER FIRST day this bloke comes in, starts reciting *Howl*. Best minds of my generation and all that.

What do you think of that then? This bloke, he has no hair, hardly any teeth, speaks rough as fuck, spits out the poetry.

Impressive, she says.

Here you are, here's some more.

He carries on, right up until about halfway through.

You don't hear that very often, she says.

We did poems at school, I never learned fuck all else but we did these poems at school and I realized I could remember them and then my wife introduced me to this poem and I read it and I remembered it, can do the whole thing if you give me a day to practice.

Don't worry about it, love.

But Ginsberg, he's one of the best. Have you got any more editions? I've had loads from here before. What's your name?

Angela.

Okay, Ange, have I seen you before?

No, I've only just started.

Is the old fella around?

Erm, not at the moment, he might come in later. I think I've seen a really old copy of that just recently, she says, and looks through the wobbly pile of books on the desk behind her.

Here, what about this one, she says, holding a battered City Lights edition.

Na, got three of them! That's what I'm saying!

Okay, she says, leafing through the book. As she does so, some pages fall out.

Ha! Ha! Ha! Well it's fucked now!

Yes, well, we can keep this between us.

No good to any fucker now!

Yeah, you have to be a bit more careful with these old ones.

Fucked anyway, nobody would have had that one off you.

True she says, dropping it into a basket under the desk. She'll put it in the shed later, and then recycling Raymond will take it after he's used the bog.

The other person works downstairs is this lad Sebastian, and she knows straight away he is right up himself. You can't give an opinion on anything without him disagreeing, and he's aloof, looks down his nose at her. Thinks he knows everything when she is knocking sixty and he looks about fucking twelve. He is a fucking vegan and all, keeps banging on about it, only has oat milk cos proper milk is cruel on the cows. Farts like a bastard. He's into music and literature and stuff, but is a snob about that as well, so that at first she thinks they might get on, but then after a while it's just pleasantries, are you having a coffee, that kind of thing, but even then you can tell that when it's his turn to brew up he doesn't like having to make one for her. She starts telling him about her band and how they knew Siouxsie and the Banshees and that, but he doesn't listen, just interrupts her and starts quoting fucking Greil Marcus and all these other music journos, doesn't give her chance to tell him that she met fucking Greil Marcus back in the day. Goes on about Scott Walker and Syd Barrett and all. Sebastian also says he comes from Glasgow, must have been the fucking posh part then, tries to make out his working-class credentials but it's a crock of shit.

Liam upstairs is a miserable old bastard, but she knows where she is with people like that. He reads Jack London. Lives quite near her and says he has this cabin he's made in the garden and he's always in there watching horror videos because he says they make him feel like he's alive, and he'll have his dog with him and he'll smoke a bit of weed cos his Mrs won't have it in the house. Liam says nobody is allowed in the cabin and she begins to wonder what he gets up to in there. But he isn't a perv or a paedo or out, she isn't saying that, she could tell he was alright and she was gonna get on with him fine.

She is still getting a bit of Universal Credit to supplement her part time work in the bookshop. She has a tiny bit of spare money to herself each week, so she can keep going to the café on her days off. They do nice coffee there and she can save on her heating, finds she's not that often in the flat except just to get home in the evening and sleep, and in the bookshop she can get first pick of anything that comes in.

She's picked up one or two great books, stuck them in her rucksack while nobody was looking. So far, she's got a Debbie Harry biography, a book on Johnny Marr, the Dylan autobiography, and it's a perk of the job seeing as though she's on minimum wage. It's a treat when she gets home and empties her rucksack and adds the second-hand books to the shelf. She's got a whole row of books yet to read and it feels good, like having something in reserve. At night instead of putting on the TV and letting her brain go to mush she reads and gets enough of a creative boost to see her through three days in work which are a piece of piss anyway.

On a good day downstairs in the shop they'll take a ton, but most days it's more like twenty. Most of the profit is made from selling books online through Abe Books and Amazon.

When Angela gets home, she takes off her trainers, makes a brew of Moroccan tea that fills the flat with the aroma of mint, drinks the brew and then gets out of her work clothes to have a shower. After the shower she smells all clean like nice new linen and sits there on the couch, one leg stretched straight across to the coffee table. She opens a book, Rimbaud poetry, fucking genius weirdo, weird systems of colours, mind blowing stuff by a guy who wrote his best stuff as a teenager. Youth is wasted on the young, not in this fucking case cos the words are ace, and she's lost in them until she gets hungry and it's time for tea and she warms up the pot of aloo gobi, and has a roti with it, fills herself, makes some more tea, fruit tea this time, blackberry, settles down with the brew.

There's never any decent looking people come in the shop, they're all either sad lonely men or fat mums coming in after dropping their bin lids off at the nearby primary school. There's one of the mums is pretty fit and Angela looks forward to her coming in, but men-wise there's nothing, they all just fucking waffle on like men do, all hot air, not a fucking listener among them, so there's no point even saying anything because when she does they don't even seem to have heard it and just go on with their fucking monologues. That was the thing with her Colin, he listened, wasn't a talker at all really. Spoke quietly and carried a big dick.

There's a load of boxes dumped in the kid's section cos a bloke came in the day before and donated a load of books, so she picks up one box and takes it to the counter before grabbing all the books out of the box and turning them face down in a pile. There's the usual stink of dust and damp. One book at a time gets checked, the ISBN number typed in, unless it's an obviously shitty book, although even then sometimes they can be worth a bit, you can't always tell, and again she checks the price other booksellers have put the book at on Abe and Amazon. As usual, if it's worth more than three quid she puts it on the system, adds it to the shop listings, makes it available online. Anything worth less she puts on the table in the shop, or in the shed for recycling Raymond. There's a load of local history pamphlets, and they are worth ten and twenty quid each. It's stuff that has a limited print run that's valuable, not your bestsellers, your *Game of Thrones*, Harry Potter, or your classics, that have been published year after year for decades. She types in the ISBN for another one of the local history booklets, *Rivers of Manchester*, sees it's worth thirty quid and adds it to the online stock, before writing the catalogue number on a post-it note and sticking the note in the front of the book. All morning she does this, and there's no customers, and there's this sad fucking classical music on the radio that Sebastian likes, but soon enough it's twelve and time for lunch. She's got leftover curry that's she's put in a blue bowl that will go in the microwave, stinking the kitchen out, so she puts it in and waits two minutes before taking it out again, grabbing a fork and taking her food back behind the counter. If there is a busy time it's at lunch, and as she sticks some of the curry into her mouth a guy comes round the corner with a pile of westerns, Larry McMurtry and that. She looks at the prices on them, tells him the total, but he's half mutton, and instead of giving her money he puts a plastic bag on the counter and says he's brought books back, so no money changes hands, the books are just swopped over. This bloke with the westerns says he is going in hospital, and it will give him something to read, so what can she do? She finishes her curry, eats an apple, puts the apple core in the bowl and puts it in the kitchen before getting another box of books and carrying on all afternoon pricing them up. There's no sense in rushing, not on minimum fucking wage, and it's like anything else, if she whizzes through them she'll have fuck all else to do until more books come in, so she takes her time, drags it out, works smart not hard.

Middle of the afternoon this bloke comes to the counter with a novel.

Will you take a pound for that?

She looks at the price, pencilled on the flyleaf. It's two fifty, she says.

I know but will you take a pound?

It's in decent nick.

Come on, it's only a small novel.

Well size isn't relevant really.

Will you take a pound?

Erm . . . you can have it for one fifty.

Here's a pound.

Oh, okay then. I'm not going to haggle over fifty p.

Great, he says, fishing a fiver out of his wallet.

Is it?

What?

Is it great? We wouldn't last long in this business if everyone was as tight as you.

What?

I said we wouldn't last long in this business if everyone was as tight as you.

She gives him the book and his change, and he walks out.

After he leaves the shop, she bobs out to put an empty cardboard box into the shed and sees the bastard in a Mercedes.

She'll remember his face, and if she's on the counter when he comes in again, he'll get fuck all out of her.

It's a funny thing, some people she gives discounts to, especially if they buy loads or are just nice. She's seen Liam and Sebastian do it. But if people come in asking for a discount or expecting one, she sticks to the price.

⁂

This woman comes to the counter and asks if they have any Helena Blavatsky. Angela has never heard of her but looks on Homebase. They've had books in the past, but don't have any in stock now. The young woman shakes her head and says it doesn't matter and then leaves the shop.

Angela looks up this Blavatsky online. She was one of these alternate history types, into the occult, mad ideas about alternative religions and that. There was a thing called Vril she was into, and that was half of how the Bovril drink got the name.

There was this other person came in, he was into Velikovsky, another fucking oddball, and he spoke about it, went on:

I had a very deep religious experience, in fact you can say I had a visit from god, and it was quite a long visit and it changed the way I think about things, and this Velikovsky, you want to look him up, said some very clever things, they make you think, and if you read it with all this shit that's going on now, he knew his stuff, he knew all this was going to happen. Have you got any David Icke? I mean, can you look him up on your system there? Nice one, anything.

She looked and they didn't have anything in stock.

Okay, doesn't matter, he said, and then after he left the

shop this other bloke came up, and he was buying a copy of *Blindness*, and he said, I overheard what you were saying there, what that bloke was saying, and I've read Velikovsky, and some of what he says is very interesting, but it's all a bit outdated now, discredited some of it. And as for David Icke, he's a bit dodgy, some of what he's doing is just wrong. I'd steer clear of that shit and if I were you, I wouldn't ever get it stocked in the shop.

She remembers these customers who come in asking for Velikovsky and David Icke and Helena Blavatsky, and she asks Liam about it as they stand outside having a fag.

They've all had drug experiences, he says, that's what it is. Believe me, I know, I've done every drug there is you can do, and when you do drugs you open up to these alternative voices, it's interesting stuff. But it hasn't aged well. I've not read much of Helena Blavatsky but I've read Velikovsky, and that guy, we've been ordering Velikovsky books for him for years.

He said he'd been visited by God.

You'd be amazed how many people have said that in here over the years.

They all been on drugs?

Well, I know the Velikovsky bloke, he was in here telling me once, and I think he had a bad acid trip, a bad experience with LSD and it fucked him up a bit.

You ever been visited by God?

Na. But anyway I never do the hard stuff. I did heroin once and I was ill for days. Mushrooms were the best, every spring we'd all go down the woods for mushrooms. You get people in here asking for guides to mushrooms, they think you don't know why. They were great though. You could just look at your face in the mirror and watch it stretching. You could stand there for hours, and your hands, you'd look at your hands and they were dripping. My Mrs still does all that kind of stuff, loves it, yet I can't have a spliff in the house. I've got some Tramadol tucked away though, that will fuck you up. But yeah, all this Velikovsky and Tesla, Tesla's another one, we get a few coming in, you'll get more coming in about it. It's cos everything is so shit. Nobody believes what they see on TV, so they want to look for something else, an alternate reality, or a conspiracy theory, and it's interesting to explore it, Twitter is fucking full of it, especially now. It's no wonder people round here are into it, but you don't have to read all that shit, just have some mushrooms and wander round Lidl off your tits.

Kevin's a regular, works at the airport doing security.

Alright if I bring you these in?

Yeah, she says.

Think there's a few quid's worth there. Is it okay if I find something else to swop for it?

No worries. She knew the score with Kevin now. They let him use it as a library cos he actually brought some decent books in sometimes. These looked good, some brand new. And a Dean Koontz one as well, *The Eyes of Darkness*.

You off work today?

Yeah.

Is it the airport you work?

That's right, yeah.

How long you been there?

Few years now.

So, it's your day off today is it?

Yeah, it's a funny shift. I do six days on then I get two days off together, but I always have to do six days first.

Sounds knackering.

It is a bit, but I'm getting used to it. It's good the airport, people moan it was all fields and that before, but the jobs are a godsend round here. Looking a bit dodgy now though. Anyway, I think I'm going to go have a look in the General Fiction.

Have you seen everything in there is a quid now?

Is it? The hardbacks as well?

Yep, everything in there a quid.

Oh, sounds good, I'll go and have a look.

He comes back in with a couple of Margaret Atwood hardbacks about ten minutes later and says if he's alright to swop them. He asks every time, and she says yes, and he says thanks, he always says thanks.

❧

This lad comes in. He's got on the kind of grey jogging pants and sweatshirt they wear in prison. The clothes stink. He's got a skinhead but looks about twelve. He says to Angela, books, yeah?

Er, yeah, books.

You got books?

Plenty.

You got that *Game of Thrones*?

Probably be one just down the next aisle there.

Which aisle?

It's just down there.

You got that Harry Potter and all?

Yes, there's one or two left.

How many books you got in here?

Half a million.

Fucking half a million? No fucking way.

Okay, more like a hundred thousand.

Where do you get them all from?

All over. People bring them in.

You give them money? I've got some old bibles.

It's very rare we pay anyone. They usually just donate them. If they're in good condition.

What if they aren't in good condition?

Then they go to the recycling.

Oh right. Langley Lane?

That's it.

Okay okay, might bring my bibles in then.

Okay, but like I say—

—Oh I know. But they are in good condition. And I wouldn't want much for them.

Okay.

So, like, what's the percentage? I mean, if I bring a bible in and you sell it for say like a tenner, how much would you pay me?

It's a buyer's market.

Eh?

Well, roughly, if we pay you a quid for a book, we will sell it for four quid, something like that. But like I say usually people just give us the books for nowt, they just want to clear a room out, spring cleaning usually, or if someone has died.

What do you mean?

Loads of times when people die the relatives will just clear out the house. Last week we had a load of books in, and they had the woman's name written on. People can't bear to just throw the books away. Good news for us when someone carks it.

Oh.

Yeah, all these psychology books, education, history. Every one of them had the name Mary Hankerson in.

Old Mary brown bread then?

It would seem so.

Good of the rellies to give you all the books.

Yes.

I'll come back with the bibles.

Next day he's in again. Drops the carrier bag on the counter, takes out these tatty old hardback bibles. Spines falling off, pages coming out.

Can't give you anything for them.

Seriously?

No.

You said to bring them in yesterday.

I said we rarely pay. You can leave them if you want, we will put them in the recycling.

Recycling? These are too good for the recycling. Come on, won't you give me anything?

We aren't buying books at the moment.

You've changed your tune since yesterday.

No I haven't.

Fucking hell.

No need for that.

What if I tell you to give me some money out of the till?

I'd tell you to fuck off out of the shop.

I don't need your shitty little shop! he shouts, so close she can feel his spit on her face. I'll go somewhere else and someone will give me decent money for these. They are antiques, you old cow.

Okay, bye then.

Yeah, fucking cheers, granny.

Embarrassing.

You're fucking embarrassing, you old cow!

He slams the door behind him before she can shout back.

When the cardboard box is emptied, Angela comes back out of the container and sees a little fella on his way into the shop. He's tiny, and he has on this sharp suit and shiny black shoes, and there's a light blue silk scarf around his neck.

Oh hello, he says.

You okay?

Yes, yes, was just passing.

Anything in particular that you're looking for?

I deal in coins.

I think we have a few coin books.

Well not books so much as ephemera, if you know what I mean.

Ephemera?

Yes, ephemera.

Na, it's just mainly books we do.

Okay, okay, he says, before smiling. I was just on my way past. Is the old man still around?

Mr Bancroft?

That's it. Is he still . . .

Yeah, he's still going strong.

Amazing. A lovely man, such a lovely man.

He was in last week. Still drives here.

Still drives? He's a lovely man, such a lovely man.

Yeah, he's eighty-three now.

Eighty-three? That's amazing. I'm eighty-one.

Right, well, it's not a competition, is it love?

No, no, ha ha. So, he's not in today?

No, sorry.

Oh, he's a lovely man, a lovely man, such a lovely man.

I've been told he's mellowed over the years.

Oh, a lovely man. Here, have a look at this, he says, hold-ing out a shiny coin. What do you think of that, he says, passing it to her.

Nice, she says, rolling it between thumb and forefinger before giving it back.

Only about twenty of them left in the world.

Amazing.

Will you be so kind as to do me a favour, he says, putting on a pair of leather driving gloves. Will you tell him Danny came in, was asking after him?

Yes, yes, will do, she says, and as he leaves, she watches him get into a white car with who she guesses is his wife. She's smiling, a bit giddy, looks about eighty as well. They've had a day out or something. The car does a three-point turn to leave the yard and as it does, she notices the side of his car where it says, *Dan, Dan, The Coin Man, Coins Bought and Sold* in black lettering.

Later in the day Coffee Table Guy turns up, looking, as

usual, for any big books that might have come in, and as always he comes at about quarter to five.

Erm, what time are you closing today?

Still five.

Have you had much new stuff come in?

Yeah, but not really any of the kind of stuff you like.

Oh right, okay, well, that's a pity then, but I will have a look around as I always seem to be able to find something if I look hard enough.

True.

So it's five?

Sorry?

Close at five.

That's right. As always.

Okay well I might go and have a look upstairs first.

Okay, she says, watching as he takes off his red woolly hat and shuffles off.

At five to five, she can still hear him wandering around upstairs.

She walks up and tells him she's closing in five minutes.

Okay, he says, I lost track of time, he says.

Liam and Sebastian have gone home, they both have buses to get before five. Angela puts away the boxes from under the awning, tugs the rope that sends up the awning, locks the containers outside, brings the sign in, and then shouts that she's closing up.

As he's coming down the stairs, she notices him squinting at a folio above the counter. It's a lovely book on Venice and he asks to look at it.

She lifts it down for him. He slides it out of the protective sleeve, opens the pages slowly. All the time Angela is looking at her watch, jangling the keys, but Coffee Table guy is oblivious. He's very quiet, stutters a bit, never gets to the point.

How much would you want for this? There's no price on it.

Let me have a look, she says. Trouble is I've turned the computers off now, so I can't check online.

That's a shame.

Yeah.

Oh well, I can maybe give you three quid for it?

No, I couldn't sell it that cheap, not without checking it. You're better off coming when the manager is in.

When is the manager in?

Tomorrow.

I could maybe give you a fiver?

Like I say, come in another time.

Coffee Table Guy starts frowning, he's not happy. She hasn't seen him react like this before.

She turns off the CCTV monitor, then the light behind the counter, moves towards the door, hopes he'll take the hint. She almost has to push him out of the door. He's not happy but she shows him out and turns off all the lights. He stands there watching as he she pulls down the shutter, locks it. It's a bit creepy, him standing there right behind her, nobody else around.

※

You go on to the Abe orders, write them down, then the same with the Amazon orders, write down the catalogue number for each on a sheet of paper, then you go and get the books, five millions or whatever and then you print off the order sheets for them and tuck them inside the books, and then you take the pile of books over to the packing desk, where you peel off the address label, stick it on the edge of the table, pack the book, stick the label on the parcel, then take it over to the scales and weigh it and list the weight and then stamp the boxes with second class or airmail or surface mail and whatever, then put the parcels in the sack before taking them downstairs. As long as you get the bag downstairs before three it's okay, because that's when the post comes. Then obviously you have to take those books off the system to show they have been sold, and then that's it, pretty straightforward, like I say not rocket science, so if I leave it with you for this morning and just give me a shout if you're struggling with anything, and then this is the thing you see, if me or Sebastian have to stay off you can come up here and do the orders, be very useful if you get the hang of it up here, like I say not rocket science. So, you know what you're doing?

I think so, cheers Liam.

Okay well what's your first number?

Five, zero, one, six, six, two, three.

Five millions, okay great that's just down there, he says, pointing.

Okay.

Don't worry you should have plenty of time to find those, and like I say you'll get more of an idea of where things are as you go along.

Okay thanks, Liam.

No problem.

2

There's always the Proust thing, says Sebastian.

What's that?

À la recherche du temps perdu?

Eh?

Remembrance of Things Past. You've heard of Proust?

Yes, I've heard of Proust.

Well there you go then.

Fuck's sake, Sebastian, what you going on about?

Have you not read about the Petite Madeleine?

What?

I can't believe you don't know about the Petite Madeleine.

You on about the cake thing?

That's correct.

Why didn't you just say that then? You don't half beat around the fucking bush, lad.

Sorry.

What about these fucking cakes then?

Well Proust made the proposition that the sumptuous taste of the cake evoked the most startling and numinous memories of his childhood, which he could then recount in the most precise and exquisite detail, and it really is marvellous, precisely because of eating the cake.

What *are* you fucking waffling on about?

Well I just thought I'd mention it.

So, what about it?

Don't know, just trying to be helpful, I guess.

How is that helpful, twatty bollocks? I can't fucking taste anything. What part of that don't you understand?

Didn't mean to upset you.

Doesn't upset me. Don't have to smell your fucking arse anymore for a start.

That's . . . that's just unnecessary.

You're fucking unnecessary at times, lad. I can't taste, I can't fucking smell. What part of that can't you understand?

There must be something on Google?

Don't you think I've looked, knobhead? Google is full of crackpots, do this, do that. And none of it fucking works. Everything tastes like fucking cardboard, that's why I don't eat, what's the point? It's just like hard work, chew, chew, chew, for fuck all, no reward for the effort, and I used to love my food and drink, and all of that is gone now. I put chilli fucking sauce on everything, fucking bucketloads of sriracha, and every time I go for a dump my shithole stings like a bastard.

Oh, dear lord. Could be worse off.

How?

Well, you could be, shall we say, no longer of this earth. Beyond this mortal coil.

Shit's sake, you talk some bollocks, lad.

I would suggest there's more to life than taste and smell. A whole panoply of senses.

Is there? Like what?

I'm just suggesting that perhaps an adaptation is in order, on your behalf. An adaptation to this unfortunate turn of events, rather than just going on some tirade at any unfortunate chap who is just trying to create a semblance of harmony in the workplace.

Go and play chicken on the motorway, lad, she says, going outside to sit in the smoking shelter.

Might as well give up, save a few quid, she mutters. Be better for the C.O.P.D.

It's only later she starts thinking about what Sebastian said. What were the other senses? Sight, touch, and hearing. Least she isn't fucking mutton jeff.

She's trying to remember them, and some of them are coming back to her, she doesn't need any petite fucking Proust cake either, and once they come the memories keep flooding in like what they called the Kingsway Stink from the glue factory where they boiled the bones of old horses, and then there was the sewage plant with the metal arm going round in a circle and all the little birds eating bits of shit, and cut grass smells from watching her brothers play cricket and all kind of cricket smells because when she remembers one thing it links in with another, triggers another one off so once she starts thinking about cricket there's the leather smell of the cricket balls where the lads licked their fingers and shined one side of the ball with spit, and then the smell of the cricket bats, the smell of that willow, and then the smell of the linseed oil that they had to oil the bats with in those days, and then the smell of whitener which was like white paint that the older players put on their boots and pads and whatever else needed whitening, she even remembers the smell of sandwiches the players had for their tea halfway through the game, and lemon drizzle cake and tea, and then the beer smells on their breath from the night before and the beer smell from the bar, and the beer smell from every gig smelling of beer and every gig smelling of the sweat of them on stage and the sweat of them in the audience, a mix of sweat and perfume and fag smoke and beer and weed and spirits, then there was the smell of chips from the chippy, the pine smell of new furniture out of a box and needing to be put together, flowers in the garden, lupins, shit like that, washing in a washing machine, that clean smell of clothes when you take them out, the fabric softener smell all over the house, toast and coffee every morning, garlic from the next door neighbour who seemed to cook with it every day so that her whole gaff smelled of it, the print smell on magazines that you don't seem to get so much anymore, that print smell that made her stick her nose in the pages and turn the pages and waft the pages, and then the salty, cheesy smell of old socks, the salty, cheesy smell of men after sex, that fishy smell of sex and salty crown jewels, stinking gonads, and then back to grass, the smell of mud on grass, the smell of puddles on grass, the smell of canals, the smell of the sea, the smell of dog shit on muddy fields, the damp fur smell of cats and dogs, the smell of chocolate when you opened a chocolate bar, the smell of fresh baking bread from the bakery that wafted in on the wind, the smell in another flat when you opened the windows, the smell of the brewery, the beer smell of the brewery, and in another flat the smell of the chocolate from the McVitie's factory churning out Jaffa cakes, and these are all things she remembers, and she gives herself a hard time for not appreciating those smells, and she thinks of the smells that other people have, that pheromone thing and she knows nothing about that now and she remembers how she liked the way her Colin smelled, which was just really the smell of weed mixed with a bit of sweat and she remembers now how that smell on the street always made her think for a split second Colin was back, and she remembers the way her babies seemed to smell like chocolate somehow.

❧

There are more donations than ever, but something is going to have to change. The online sales don't even cover the wages of the two of them. It's fucking bitter too, sometimes the containers and the shop feel colder that it is outside, the containers can stay cold for months and months. She has the little oil heater on under the counter to keep her legs warm, and there's the two-bar fire behind her. Fucking great them two bar fires, give off some serious heat, and she remembers how they used to have one when she was a kid and her mum would light fags on it, a little burn mark briefly on the bar and then the stench of the B & H filling the air. She knows they cost a mint but on days like these when she's just sat behind the counter and there's a massive draft coming in through the shutters, she needs it on. She's sat there wearing thermals, a fleece, a woolly hat, and she still needs the leccy fire and the oil heater on or else she gets fucking brassic.

Sebastian asks her if she wants a coffee, he's got some proper coffee if she wants to try some. She says she will, though it's futile. Coffee, like everything else, doesn't really taste of anything anymore. But after a few minutes, she looks up from the book she's reading, then shouts, as loud as she can, I can smell it! I can smell it! It fucking reeks you knobhead!

Ghosteen

WHEN WINNIE SAID she'd lost a child in the house in which I lived it seemed to confirm a feeling about the place I'd previously tried to dismiss. Like the lake by the sawmill and the wreckage of old houses on the hills, I felt, in both the landscape and the buildings, something lingering, some remnant of the life passed still clinging to the wind blasted surrounds.

Once I'd been in a marriage. If we'd had another child maybe that would have changed everything, maybe we would have mellowed, stopped sniping, grown together in the glow of our new offspring. At least Winnie had her other children, her husband, her job, a whole routine of life shaped around her shifts at the petrol station.

I followed the path where the railway had been, cut through the campsite and saw a large crowd of people drinking beer behind a circle of wind breaks. They threw empty cans onto a blazing bonfire, and they laughed, the men scratching bare chests and roaring at each other's jokes.

When I passed them their talk subsided somewhat, then went quiet altogether, like I'd walked into a country pub as a stranger. One of them shouted that I should come over and have a beer, but when I politely declined, thinking I needed to get back home, there was a grumbling, and the same voice said, *well fuck you then*, and there was laughter, and the noise of talking rose back up, and I was glad to pass through the campsite and be on my way.

Approaching a crossroads, I turned and saw two men behind me in the darkness. They sensed my fright and laughed. They took a left along the road heading back to the campsite. I'd been planning to take the path, but I stayed on the road and followed the chevrons in the moonlight, looking behind me all the while, jumping when a pheasant leapt from a bush. I passed beyond the turn off and the lake. I heard the low rumble of traffic and looked across the valley towards the sparkling headlights on the A road. I passed the big hall and the farm there, returning to where my rented house sat quiet and still, the dark living room window reflecting the solitary street light above the post box.

One afternoon I crossed a wobbly wooden stile and looked out across the slanted ground. At first there seemed to be nothing there. But as I walked diagonally across the field, from one stile to another, I almost trod on something fragile. I walked on carefully, observantly, especially around tussocks and tufts. I looked down and saw a little circle of straw and a bundle of beige eggs with darker blotches on. When I crouched over the eggs the lapwings wheeled hysterically.

As I walked slowly away, I took the binoculars out of my rucksack and scanned the field to capture in the glasses the birds whose calls rang across the air. Looking towards the burn at the bottom of the field I saw two curlews gliding one way then another, all the time filling a space in the sky with their calls; calls that seemed to echo back and forth as though from inside a great chamber.

When I got home from the pub, I went into the bedroom I'd decorated. I ripped down the curtains and scratched at the walls, tipped over a wardrobe and wrenched up the corners of the carpet. I woke the following morning on the floor, hugging a small pillow, with a pile of vomit beside the bed.

I puked again until I thought I would rip my own stomach out. Eventually it subsided. I walked very slowly across the room, trying to keep my head at the same level, then lowered myself onto the bed and lay back. Lying there I concentrated on not vomiting again. I couldn't move without feeling awful, so I lay as motionless as possible and when it eventually started to get dark, got up, dressed myself and went down to the kitchen for coffee.

I stood on the front doorstep for some air. It was totally dark apart from the street light above the post box. All was silent save the occasional vehicle along the A road. I looked up at the common and it was covered in low mist, a mist that mingled with the smoke pouring from the chimneys of the other houses. I looked up at the moon and it seemed yellowed by the smoke. I walked into the yard and could see into the front room of my neighbour. Winnie sat watching TV with her husband Richard, a shepherd on the estate.

※

I was lying in bed, under all the covers I needed to keep me warm, listening to the dull hammering that seemed to come from underground that I guessed was machinery at the nearby container plant. The moonlight shone through the thin brown curtains that were inadequate for keeping out light and keeping in warmth. As the beams of moonlight shone on the long lumps of my legs, I heard the crying of a child; desperate crying for attention, or crying caused by pain, I couldn't tell which. It subsided into a consistent, steady crying, lower in volume. This quiet crying went on and on, muffled by the walls, accompanied by the moonlight and the silence of the moorland outside. I scratched my nose but it was ice cold and I put my hand quickly back under the covers. A strange shadow had formed behind the curtains in the moonlight. I got up and reached between the curtains. I didn't have my glasses on, so it was a moonlit blur. I touched the window and there was something there; something growing, something cold. I ran my hand along its forming ridges and the cold ran up my arm. The child was still quietly crying. I snatched my hand back through the curtains and went to the toilet and, as I stood there, looked at the bathroom window which also had something growing on it. I reached out with my free hand to touch it and again it was ice cold. I turned on the tap in the sink to wash my hands and no water came out and still the child was quietly crying. There was a sudden and all-pervading smell of coal-tar soap. I felt my way along the walls of the corridor and then got back into bed, pulling the heavy covers over me, my body shivering beneath them.

Talking to Winnie one morning before she drove off for her shift at the petrol station, I asked her about the campsite in the hills.

You know what, I've never been along the road that way, she said.

So, in all the time you've lived here you've never been up there?

No. I've known people who go fishing up there. Have you been to the lake?

Yeah, it is lovely up there. You should go for a walk. But I don't recommend the campsite.

Why do you need to camp?

I don't, I'm just talking about the campsite. Have you never heard of it?

I think my Richard knows them up there. But I'd never go camping. I don't like confined spaces.

Seems a strange place.

I've never been up there so I couldn't tell you. I don't know anything about it. I will tell you something though. I won't walk my dog in that field, she said, pointing across the car park towards a field that led to a forest. I had a dog once that got poisoned from taking it into that field. He's the man who owns the house you're living in. Owns all the houses in the village. They've owned the land for years and years. You know the big hall? Have you seen it? Well, they use half of that for conferences and things now, but he lives there. People say he lets jackdaws in through the windows. My Richard works for him on the farm. George doesn't do anything, just takes the rent.

In the evening I walked down the road in the darkness. Highland cattle were motionless in the field. Light from the hall windows spread across the grounds, illuminating tumbled stonework. I could hear the river close by. Pine plantations on the hillsides were silhouettes on the night sky. I walked around the curve of the road past the forest that gave the hall shelter from the wind. I could hear my own footsteps on the tarmac. Half of the house was in darkness. I saw gargoyles staring from the rooftops. There was a tipped over trampoline in the grounds before the window, a moon-lit tennis court with a collapsed net and a solitary ball in the corner. Some of the unlit windows I could see had cracks in them, others were boarded up entirely. Bats spiralled past me in the darkness. In the white light beyond the windows, I saw something black and flying and an old man with his arms in the air who looked like he was preaching. Then the bird landed on the arm of the old man and he put it into a tall cylindrical cage. I watched as the old man shuffled from one brightly lit room to another. In the living room he went to a glass cabinet and poured himself a glass of something before returning to sit in a chair by the birdcage. I heard a solitary sheep in a distant field, the brief sharp disturbance of an oystercatcher from the riverbank, pheasants in the field closer. As I walked back past the highland cattle, the two of them were just hulks in the field, motionless either side of the feeder. I looked back towards the hall and saw shifting shadows across the light on the lawn, as though there were people in one part of the hall enjoying each other's company while George sat alone in another. I left the shadows on the lawn behind and carried on back up the road in the darkness. Dark blue stretches of night sky were filled with black clouds.

꧁

That night I was woken by barking. I jumped out of bed to look through the curtains, but all was darkness outside. I looked at my watch and it was ten past two. I went back to sleep, and the barking came again. I checked the time, and it was ten past three. Again, there was nobody to be seen outside. This second barking was a little more disturbing but after what must have been an hour I went back to sleep. Within five minutes another loud barking woke me up. It was ten past four. I still couldn't see anything outside the window and this time around my heart was racing. I dressed and went downstairs and walked out of the front door to stand in the yard and look around but there was nothing there.

In the morning I waited for Winnie before she got in her car to go to the petrol station.

Hi, Winnie, I said, did you hear any barking last night?

Barking? What time? No, I didn't hear any barking.

You didn't hear any barking?

No, I didn't. Anyway, I've got to get to work, she said, closing her car door.

For the next week, my sleep remained undisturbed, and the barking went from my mind. But a week to the day it resumed. This time the first barking came at a quarter past eleven, not long after I'd gone to bed. I leapt from the bed and darted to the window but as usual I couldn't see anything outside. I kept myself awake for the next hour, peeping through the curtains. Twelve fifteen came and there was no barking, by twelve thirty still nothing. I drifted off to sleep and within a few minutes there was a loud barking again.

The barking started to happen almost every night. I went out walking in the afternoons and it felt like I was sleepwalking across the fields. It was on the last of these walks that I came down off the hillside above the hall and paused to see Winnie staring into my windows. I asked her what she was doing but she just walked away.

On my last morning the house was surrounded by mist. I opened the front door and looked down to see what seemed like paw prints beginning on the doorstep and continuing across the car park. I walked over to the field where the paw prints became indentations on the grass and followed them through the mist into the forest, where I glanced up and saw a child hanging from the trees.

Acknowledgements

S OME OF THESE stories first appeared (in slightly different form, some with different titles) in *Cōnfingō*, *The Manchester Fiction Prize Shortlist 2020*, *Murmurations*, *Nightjar Press*, *Outsideleft*, *Short Fiction Journal*, *The Lonely Crowd* and *Unthology 6*. My thanks to the editors. Thanks are also long overdue to the Society of Authors for their Authors' Foundation award. This grant, the only one I've ever received in twenty years as a writer, came at a time of financial insecurity, and was a great help in the completion of this book.

This book has been typeset by
SALT PUBLISHING LIMITED
using Granjon, a font designed by George W. Jones
for the British branch of the Linotype company in the
United Kingdom. It is manufactured using Holmen
Bulky News 52gsm, a Forest Stewardship Council™
certified paper from the Hallsta Paper Mill in Sweden.
It was printed and bound by Clays Limited in Bungay,
Suffolk, Great Britain.

CROMER
GREAT BRITAIN
MMXXII